THE INNOCENT AND THE GUILTY

THE INNOCENT AND THE GUILTY

STORIES BY

SYLVIA TOWNSEND WARNER

NEW YORK · THE VIKING PRESS

First published in 1971 by The Viking Press, Inc.
625 Madison Avenue, New York, N.Y. 10022

SBN 670-39837-3
Library of Congress catalog card number: 76-104138

Printed in U.S.A.

The following stories originally appeared in *The New Yorker:*
"Truth in the Cup," "But at the Stroke of Midnight," "A Visionary
Gleam," "The Perfect Setting," "The Green Torso," and "Oxen-
hope."

 CONTENTS

THE INNOCENT AND THE GUILTY

TRUTH IN THE CUP

Jim Ridley heard his Janey's voice sound out like a foghorn. "They go to one of these hard-stuff parties. They get hooked —and they're done for. Done for! Done for!"

The invitation cards read, "Village Get-Together. 9 p.m. onward." Everyone had arrived more or less simultaneously. The drinks were on the house. Drinking whenever the trays went round as the sand drinks the waves, they were now in the moral stage of tipsiness.

"A whole generation gone down the drain. It's too awful, really."

"Something ought to be done about it."

"But what? It's gone too far. Think of the profits."

"It's the parents I blame."

"Yes, I blame the parents, too. No discipline."

The moral roar extended as a toppling wave runs along the beach. At one extremity Topsy Mainwaring was declaiming about long-haired lay-abouts. At the other, old Bilby's shrill voice reiterated a demand for a good old-fashioned whacking. Janey brisked up and called across the room, "Now, Bibbles, you'd better be careful. We all know the sort of books you read."

There was laughter. The haze of tobacco smoke eddied. Belatedly, Bilby answered back. "What about you, Janey? You've no time for *reading*."

The hotel lounge was in its winter dimensions. The glass doors between it and the solarium facing seaward were closed. Thick curtains were drawn across them. The last inrush of living air, which had accompanied the arrival of the last guests —the Trubigs, she in mink, he in a fisherman's jersey, and both exclaiming, as most of the others had done, "What weather! God help those at sea!"—was a thing unrecallable. The hotel, a modern building, was draftproof and almost soundproof. Built at the sea's edge, it rose above it like a liner: a liner stranded upright and intact at the foot of the steep descent to the cove. So it was by some residual seafaring attentiveness that Jim Ridley knew that the wind had shifted and now lay full behind the making tide.

Another round of drinks was carried in—this time without complement of canapés and little toothpicked sausages. Provisions must have run out. The servants carrying the trays were making no pretense at affability. Their faces were expressionless. Even when Hermione Straker fell on her knees before Mrs. Trubig, crying, "Darling, darling, you're so witty I worship you," straight in the headwaiter's path, he skirted round her with no acknowledgment except that he skirted. It was hopeless to listen for what might be going on outside, so Jim gave his attention to old Mrs. Saunders, who was leaning cozily against him like a drunken rhesus monkey.

"Such a pleasant evening. I'm glad I had my hair done. It costs fifteen shillings now at Marina's, but I'm glad I had it done."

"It looks very nice," he said, surveying the white sprigs and the pink scalp beneath them. No one knew how old she was; only that long, long ago she had been the wife of the rector.

"I'm so glad you think so. You really are a great dear—so much nicer than Janey. I'm afraid she's had too much, poor Janey. Do you know, I can drink any man under the table?"

Looking up at him with confiding blue eyes, she filched away his glass.

They were sitting on a banquette with their backs to the dividing glass doors. The wind had certainly changed. An icy air sifted through the heavy curtains. They suddenly bellied, and at the same moment there was a sound like a thump; and another, and another. But if one of the solarium windows had been blown in, the noise of the waves, the boom and crash and snarl as they broke against the pebble bank, would have drowned all indoor noises. He glanced round to see if any of the others had noticed the thumps. They were flushed, variously animated, totally uninterested. He looked at his watch. The drinking had gone on longer than he supposed.

Longer than its source and provider had reckoned for, too. Light as a wafer, pale as gin, a queer, and probably dauntless as a lion, Colin Dudevant, the hotel proprietor, was now mincing among his guests, hoping they were enjoying themselves and rather abstractedly receiving their assurances that they were. "Our little village get-together," he repeated, while his eyes wandered in pursuit of some sign that the get-together might be preparing to break up.

It was forty years since Crickhellow had been a village, since women in aprons had helped to haul working boats up the slipway, since the Methodist Chapel had resounded with

> Oh hear us when we cry to thee
> For those in peril on the sea

sung by those whom the sea impartially fed and imperiled, since only The King of Mexico was licensed to sell intoxicating liquors and only the post office and Prospect House took summer visitors. The visitors who came because Crickhellow was cheap were replaced by others who could afford to. Hotels were built. The steep descent to the cove lost its functional garnish of rusty cans, fish heads, sauce bottles, cabbage stumps, old shoes, broken gramophone discs, flock mattresses, and blue enamel saucepans with holes in them. These were buried, and above their pits rose ranks of holiday cottages, all very individual and increasingly unlike cottages, whose inhabitants came to relax or retire from making money elsewhere, and were villagers only in a xenophobic determination to keep out caravans and coach parties, which would quite ruin the place and endanger summer rentals. This did not prevent them from accepting Colin Dudevant's collective term of "the villagers." And as old Mrs. Saunders was the only indigenous villager remaining, they might as well be called that as anything. "Sweet of you all to come on a night like this," he said now. "I'm expecting the roof to go at any moment." If he thought they'd take the hint, he was mistaken. They assured him that weather meant nothing to them, and waited for the stirrup cup.

Some, to pass the time of waiting, rose sprawlingly to their feet and began to dance. Janey came across the room and said, "Come on, Jim." She was as drunk as the others but carried her liquor with a swagger he had to admire. Thinking "Now why the hell does she want to dance with me, she must have been up to something I didn't notice," he nevertheless enjoyed the feeling of her handsome well-kept body and admired the taunting carriage of her head as they moved among the other couples. Then, both at once, Bilby and Dan Black cut in. After a derisive hesitation she went off with Bilby, with a glance at the other which told Jim all he needed to know.

But there had been something else he wanted to know—something of sharper interest, though equally beyond his control. At a swoop in the music the question came back. Yes, that was it: What the devil was going on outside?

He edged his way toward the entrance; it was a double door, with a space between. As he pushed, he noticed that the glass panel was uncommonly cold; also, that he had to push quite hard. It was water he had been pushing against, and it swirled in over the carpet of the lounge. Silently and expeditiously, he closed the inner door behind him, startled back into the guilty sensations of childhood, when he was clumsy, spilled things, trod them in with his feet, and was scolded for that, too. The water between the two doors was ankle-deep. No treading that in. He pushed the outer door. An eddy of wind caught it and almost wrenched it away from him, till the strong pressure of water closed it behind him. "Quite a flood," he muttered to himself. If he had shouted the words, they would have gone for nothing in that uproar of wind and things banging and clattering and the slap and hiss of water all around. He waded farther, and rose on the level of a terraced flower bed, where he clung to a palm tree and looked about him. There was water up to the hubs of the parked cars. They wobbled and sidled as if complying with some grotesque ceremonial of politeness. His own car was among them, but he threw the thought of it away; it was merely an item in a comic spectacle presented for his solitary entertainment. Then, looking beyond the cars, he saw a tumbling ridge of surf and that it was continuous and was surf, not spray. The sea had broken the pebble bank, battering it with those thumps, mining it with the undertow. Now, with the wind behind it and the moon beckoning it, it was flowing in so fast that angry ripples broke against him, drenching him to the knees. He ought to go back to the hotel; at least it would give Dudevant a chance to clear things from the ground floor. But before involving himself in breaking the news and being useful he wanted to have a full view of what was happening. From where he stood, this was not possible; the hotel, so artlessly lit up, intervened. He let go of the palm tree. Wading with small steps along the terraced border, shrugging his shoulders against the wind and the driven sand which peppered his face, he got beyond the screening hotel, took a firm hold of his balance, and looked full seaward. A gust of wind almost felled him. He was down on all fours, his hands insanely clutching a submerged geranium.

But as he went down he had seen something else—a burst of spray gesturing like an arm, shooting up from where no wave should be. Raising himself, he waited to see if it came again. For a while, it didn't, and he dismissed the idea that the waves were forced up the narrow slipway by the pressure of a larger breakthrough to the westward. There was another burst of spray; and then another. Something hit him a blow on the head, and at the same moment he was blinded and throttled by a bandaging embrace. It was a tangle of seaweed, wrenched up by the waves, plucked and whirled onward by the wind: the pebbled root had struck him, the long, tough, sinuous thongs fastened round him. He realized it perfectly well. He was startled, disconcerted, perhaps a trifle stunned; but he was not frightened. He was not frightened because he was in panic, divorced from the reasonability of fear. The atrocious raw smell of the sea flayed his nostrils. Each time he peeled off a thong with cold, incompetent hands the wind whipped it round him again. He lost his footing, and it seemed to him that he was falling, bound and blinded, into a depth where he would drown.

The splash of his fall and the fact that in struggling back to his feet he had turned round loosened the weed's hold, and the wind bore it off like a cloak. He saw it go. He saw a volley of spray exploding above the slipway wall, and the light over the hotel gateway showed him waves cresting round the lower gatepost and the ripples thrust upward along the ascending road. He was running. He seemed to be lifting a hundred-weight of water with each stride. His shoes came off. As he ran past the gateway, a black bulk made toward him and was stopped short, like a bull on a chain. The sea boiling in the slipway had turned one of the tethered boats upside down. He escaped it and ran on, two legs and a bursting heart. With astonishment and disbelief he found he was running on the hard dry surface of the road. He limped to a stop and sat down with his head between his hands.

When his senses came back to him, he seemed to be in another world. It was peopled by the quiet shapes of the holiday cottages. To the left was The Haven, and beyond The Haven Tintagel; to the right Woollands, Topsails, and Telescopes. Behind Woollands was View Halloo. All were empty; the villagers were either down at the party or away on cruises. It was as though he sat on a hillside among a flock of sleeping sheep. The horizon had risen with him. The sea was a vast expanse of calm flatness, unaffected by what might be going on at its margin. The wind blew, but struck less cold up here, and after the inversion of light from reflecting water underfoot the natural darkness was soothing. He began to drowse, was halfway into a dream, when a sensation of being looked at woke him. The moon had emerged from the web of hurrying cloud. Shrunken by the wind, wizened and doting, the moon looked like Mrs. Saunders. That old cockleshell craft was not likely to ride out the night, he thought. The contour of the road prevented him from seeing more than the roof of the hotel. He presently got up with a groan and dragged himself on to View Halloo and climbed the steps to its lookout.

There was no trace of the pebble bank. The slipway was a darkened swirl of current with some bobbing objects in it. The cottages beyond, his own among them, had their enviable sea views at window level. The sea was all round the hotel. The liner was afloat—a gallant sight, with its lighted windows reflected in water, its freight of expensive drunks. By now they must know what had hit them. He pictured them rushing from window to window, deriding each other, blaming each other, wailing for their cars, demanding that someone should do something, jostling on the stairs. . . .

All at once, the lights went out.

There was nothing he could do; he wasn't among them, his position was invidious, he had lost his shoes, it was midnight, there was no one about, and if there had been, no practical good could have come of it. There they were and there they would have to stay. Janey would be making the best of it in a hotel bedroom with Dan Black. Here was he—in a sense the sole survivor. When the story was told, another of the screamingly funny Crickhellow classics, he would project from it—unfavorably. If he really valued his good name, he would now disappear; hide in one of the disused tin-mine workings, steal out by night to eat raw turnips, grow a long beard, dress himself off a scarecrow, begin a new life with the Salvation Army. Meanwhile his shoes would have been found, his death by drowning established. He did not value his good name to quite that extent; yet he would like to do something on its behalf—some manly deed; some demonstration of presence of mind, some token of good will. What was that rhyme in curly lettering over his mother's desk? "Kindness in another's trouble, Courage in your own." Of course! His part was obvious. He would report it. Courage, certainly, considering the state of his feet.

Briskly, considering the state of his feet, he walked the further two hundred yards to the public telephone box. When he opened the door the light went on in a way which charmed him. The floor was dry, the atmosphere all stuffiness and seclusion. "FOR AN EMERGENCY CALL INSERT NO MONEY." Directions read many times while grubbing in his pockets for change, but till now theoretical. He dialed 999.

A mild inland voice told him it was the exchange, inquired what he wanted, asked him to speak up, please. When he did not speak up, it repeated the request. The fact was, he ought to have thought it out beforehand, and rehearsed his utterance. All that sea water and running uphill would impede any man's utterance. Here he was, by now as sober as a judge, acting with presence of mind yet unable to put one word after another. This would not do.

"I'm Crickhellow 626," he said. "Can you hear me?"

The inland voice encouraged him to go ahead. After a pause, it offered him alternatives of the Fire Brigade, the Police, the Ambulance Service. None of these seemed perfectly to apply. But it wouldn't do to sound unappreciative.

"It's hard to say. You see, the sea's broken in."

"Thieves breaking in? Then it's the police you want."

"I didn't say 'thieves.' I said 'sea.' The sea has broken in."

Feeling that he couldn't improve on this statement, he put back the receiver and lay down on the floor. The space was constricted, the floor not particularly clean. But it was warmer here than outside. He had been through a lot and needed to sleep it off.

TWO CHILDREN

During the night the easterly gale had blown itself out. For three days it had screeched over the flint-built Norfolk fishing village. Now everything looked gentle and smiling, and the blown sand plastered on windows and seaward-facing tarred walls had an air of partaking in the general relief by adding a sparkle—as though it were a cake decoration. Only the noise of the breakers perpetuated the force of the gale, filling the air with a sullen, continuous rumble. As the two children stood on the doorstep with the expanse of the school holiday before them, Johnnie said to his sister Bella, "Listen to them waves. That sound more like a railway train."

Their grandmother came out behind them. Her eye roved over the sagging fence, the sand plastered on everything, the puddle round the water butt, a bit of wet sacking entangled in the gooseberry bush. She hadn't properly finished the spring cleaning and now there was all this outside work added to it. She fetched the children's outdoor clothes and tied a handkerchief over Bella's flaxen curls. "Go you down to the beach," she said. "Tide's going out and now's the time to stock up woodhouse again."

Johnnie had an idea. He had had it for some time, now it boiled up in him. "Why can't we go on the heath? There's wood there, too."

"Go on the heath? You'll do no such thing. Why, there's great old vipers on the heath, and if one of them bit you, you'd fare to die. No! Off with you to the beach. And I don't want you back till dinnertime."

It is the unknown we fear. Ellen Hodds had lost at different times a husband, two sons and an uncle by drowning. No member of the family had ever died of snakebite. She watched the children set off along the sandy track across the dunes, dragging the homemade cart behind them, and went indoors with a quiet mind.

They heard the door slam. Johnnie paused, and looked round cautiously. Then without a word he turned and set off inland for the heath.

"You'll catch it," said his sister.

"She won't know."

"That she will. She'll know by the wood. It will be different wood."

"Shan't get any wood. We'll go on the beach after."

Their father had been one of the drowned sons. Wearing heavy seaboots, he was tossed off the deck of a herring drifter by a sudden lurch of the boat over a sandbank, and the sea swallowed him within sight of his native village. The *Hopeful Star* put in at the nearest port to tell the news, and went on after the others, the crew depressed by a limping start and a bad omen. The fishing fleet was making the long summer trip to Icelandic waters, they would not be back for several months. By then, the edge of his family's grief for Beauty Hodds would be blunted; it would be the accustomed, acquiescing grief of a fishing community, a traditional wearing like the black shawls the older women threw over their heads when they went out early in the morning to feed the hens.

Within a year of Beauty's death, his widow married again. She married an outsider, an engineer from Coventry, whom she had met while working at the Holiday Camp. He had been offered a job in Venezuela. She went with him, saying that when they were settled in a house she would come back and fetch the children. She sent money regularly and asked for photographs, but never reappeared, and the children lived on with their grandmother. Bella was the elder. She could remember her father, and remembered him even when she had forgotten her mother; he had made a pet of her, and his long absences at sea had given him a rarity value. Johnnie, two years younger, remembered neither parent. He loved his grandmother, the dog at the village shop, and, from afar, Miss Worsley, the rector's sister.

Presently, Bella began to talk. "I'm not afraid of the heath. I've often been there."

"When?

"Often and often. When you were a baby. My Daddy used to take me there. And there were ever so many vipers. But we weren't afraid. My Daddy said to them, 'You just bugger off.' "

"You oughtn't to say that."

"I didn't neither. My Daddy did."

She was a grueling companion, and he wished he had come without her. As though reading his thought, she said, "Next year, I'll go to confirmation class, and be done in Yarmouth by a bishop. In a veil. And after that I'll go with the big girls, with Doreen Pitcher and Rowena Crask. And I won't have no kid brother tagging round after me, nor you won't catch me on the heath. *What's that?*"

"A bit of old rope."

Having looked searchingly all round her, she said, "I'm tired. Let's sit down."

"Why, we aren't as much as on the heath yet."

"We'll pretend we are. We'll pretend it's a very dark night, and that it's snowing, and that we've lost our way. I'm a princess, see, and you're a page, holding my train. And you say, 'I'm so frightened, I darsn't go on.' And I say . . .'"

He sat staring at the heath, his desire probing into it, beyond the ungainly tufts of furze and the birch coppice glittering in the sunlight. A gull cried overhead, and behind Bella's scatter of words was the continuous harsh rumble of the waves. If only he could have come alone! If only she would leave off talking! He rolled over on his stomach. When you lie on your face, things sound different: the noise of the waves was now on top of him. He burrowed his forefinger into the sandy earth, delved a hole, put his nose to it and snuffed. The act reminded him of Bingo, the dog at the shop. Bingo would have dug a hole in no time, his front paws lashing, the earth flying up all round. Then he would sink his nose, give a long, exploring, ecstatic snuff, raise his head, his velvety muzzle all powdered with earth, take a firmer stance with his hind legs, and fall to digging again. Bingo's father was Mr. Larter the gamekeeper's retriever, and he was a nice dog, too; but nothing to Bingo. When Bella was confirmed and going with the big girls he would go for long walks alone with Bingo. But it couldn't be yet. Bella was forever talking about that confirmation and how she would wear a veil and buy a pair of falsies with her savings-bank money, but it was all her romancing. She was eleven, no bishop would do a girl of eleven, they had to be over thirteen. If he were with Bingo now, they would be right on the heath, beyond the birch coppice, away from the noise of the sea and hearing the sounds of inland: the swish of bracken, the rattle of holly leaves, the quick flutter of small birds. He knew what it would be like because the stranger schoolmaster last summer had twice taken them there for nature walks. But he had never managed to get there alone— and he wasn't alone now.

Bella was still talking. "What I would really like would be a budgie. I would have a gold cage for it, with a swing and a looking-glass, and I would teach it to say 'Bella,' and 'Hustle Up' and 'Pretty Budgie-Boy.' Things that Gran wouldn't be old-fashioned about, not like that parrot at The Three Mariners. And I would make it so fond of me that it would sit on my shoulder wherever I went, and come when I whistled."

The sea was still resounding, though now it had a different voice for the tide was at the ebb and the waves fell on sand instead of on pebbles.

"Whatever are you doing, Johnnie? Digging for pignuts? Going to Australia? Sit up and say something, do. You'll catch cold, lying sprawled out on the ground. Then it'll all come out, where we've been. And I shall be blamed for it. I shouldn't wonder if I'm not catching a cold myself, sitting here all this time waiting for tomorrow to be yesterday. Then it'll be bronchitis. When I was a baby I nearly died of bronchitis. For three Sundays I was prayed for in church and Reverend Worsley— What's that noise?"

"Larks."

"Don't you tell me it's larks."

Listening, she was silent for at least a minute. Then she loosened the handkerchief to sit more becomingly, pulled at some curls. "Come on! Whatever it is, we aren't going to stay here any longer. Come on, hurry up! Johnnie, do you hear me? We're not going to stay in this God-Help-Us place another minute. Nor you won't catch me here again, I can tell you that. I only did it to please you. Come on down to the beach. We've got that wood to get."

She set off, retracing the way they had come by. Passing the coil of old rope she paused and looked at it attentively. Then she gave it a kick, and quickened her pace to a run; he came after, trundling the little cart. It was not till they were among the dunes that she slowed down and began to talk about the lumps of amber which the sea might have cast up, and of what she would do with them. "And mind you look too, instead of mooning. There'll still be lots of time for the wood."

"Most of it will be toothbrushes and ketchup bottles," he said, being more cognizant of what is cast up by a storm than she.

They clambered up from the shelter of the last sand hill. The roar of the waves, the smell of salt, assailed them. The gray pebble bank, the sand beyond, the spray twirling like a rope along the line of the breakers, extended on either hand as far as the eye could reach.

"Look! Look, Johnnie!"

The austere beach was dotted with flecks of alien brilliant color.

"Oranges," he said.

"Yes. And there'll be folks after them. Hurry!"

They ran plungingly down the sand hill, the marram grass stinging their legs. Johnnie picked up an orange and bit into it. "It's sour."

"Of course it is. They're Seville oranges, for making marmalade. That'll keep Gran busy."

He picked up another. It squelched between his fingers. "This here's rotten."

"Never mind if it is. It'll do for something. Oh for goodness' sake, child, don't stand there arguing. Pick them up, hurry before other folks get them all. They're at it already, farther along."

He had seen the group of men, farther along the beach, and had seen that they were standing motionless. A deep-rooted recognition rose slowly into his mind. The dark, huddled object, prostrate among the standing men, was a body, was a drowned man whom the tossing sea had tired of and cast on shore.

"What are you staring at now? Get on with the oranges. Pile them up. Here's a beauty. Them as Gran don't want, we'll sell. We'll dress up as gypsies and cycle into Henham and sell them for a penny each. Johnnie! Do you hear me? What's come over you?"

"None of your business," he said.

"None of my business?"

She reared up in astonishment, shook the curls out of her eyes, looked where he was looking. Her eyes darkened, her jaw dropped.

"Oh no! Oh, don't say it. It's just a seal they're looking at, just a dead seal."

He began to walk toward the group of men. She ran after him, clutched his arm. "Don't go! I won't have it. Gran wouldn't never allow it. And I'll tell her. Besides, they don't want you. They don't want a kid interfering, whatever it is."

He drove his elbow into her and freed himself.

"And it's nothing but a seal, anyhow, a dead seal."

"Then get you on with your oranges."

He was astonished to hear himself speaking so harshly, and the dialect so strong in his voice.

"I won't. If you're going, I'm coming too. To look after you. I won't be left. Johnnie, Johnnie, I don't want to be left alone."

He turned and saw her furious suppliant face, and how she glanced this way and that, as though at any moment more bodies might be cast up.

"I tell you, I won't have you go. You're to stay here with me, and do as I say. I'm two years older than you, I know what's best, I—"

"You bugger off," he said. He saw her face contort for tears, and walked on with a firm tread to join the men.

BUT AT THE STROKE
OF MIDNIGHT

She was last seen by Mrs. Barker, the charwoman. At ten minutes to eleven (Mrs. Ridpath was always punctual, you could
set your watch by her) she came into the kitchen, put on the
electric kettle, got out the coffeepot, the milk, the sugar, the
two pink cups and saucers, the spoons, the coffee canister. She
took the raisin cake out of the cake tin, cut two good slices,
laid them on the pink plates that went with the two cups,
though not a match. The kettle boiled, the coffee was made.
At the hour precisely the two women sat down to their elevenses. It was all just as usual. If there had been anything not just
as usual with Mrs. Ridpath, Mrs. Barker would certainly have
noticed it. Such a thing would be quite out of the common; it
would force itself on your notice. Mrs. Ridpath was never
much of a talker, though an easy lady to talk to. She asked
after Mrs. Barker's Diane and David. She remarked that people in the country would soon be hearing the first cuckoo.
Mrs. Barker said she understood that the Council were poison-
ing the poor pigeons again, and together they agreed that
London was no longer what it was. Mrs. Barker could remember when Pimlico was a pleasure to live in—and look at it
now, nothing but barracks and supermarkets where they
treated you with no more consideration than if you were a
packet of lentils yourself. And at eleven-fifteen she said she

must be getting on with her work. Later, while she was polishing the bath, she saw Mrs. Ridpath come out of the bedroom and go to the front door. She was wearing her gray and had a scarf over her head. Mrs. Barker advised her to put on a mac, for it looked like rain. Mrs. Ridpath did so, picked up her handbag, and went out. Mrs. Barker heard the lift come up and go down, and that was the last she knew. It was Saturday, the day when she was paid her week's money, and she hung about a bit. But Mrs. Ridpath didn't come back, and at a quarter past one she left. Her credit was good, thank God! She could manage her weekend shopping all right, and Mrs. Ridpath would pay her on Monday.

On Monday she let herself in. The flat was empty. The Aga Cooker was stone-cold, the kitchen was all anyhow; the milk bottles hadn't been rinsed, let alone put out. The telephone rang, and it was Mr. Ridpath, saying that Mrs. Ridpath was away for the weekend.

By then, Aston Ridpath was so determined that this must be so that when Mrs. Barker answered him he waited for a moment, allowing time for her to say that Mrs. Ridpath had just come in.

For naturally, when he got home from his office on Saturday (the alternate Saturday when he worked during the afternoon), he expected to find Lucy in the flat, probably in the kitchen. There was no Lucy. There was no smell of cooking. In the refrigerator there was a ham loaf, some potato salad, and the remains of the apple mousse they had had on Friday. It was unlike Lucy not to be there. He turned on the wireless for the six o'clock news and sat down to wait. By degrees an uneasiness and then a slight sense of guilt stole into his mind. Had Lucy told him she would not be back till after six? He had had a busy day; it might well have slipped his memory. It was even possible that she had told him and that he had not attended. It was easy not to attend to Lucy. She had a soft voice, and a habit of speaking as if she did not expect to be attended to. Probably she had told him she was going out to tea, or something of that sort. She sometimes went to picture galleries. But surely, if she had told him she would not be back in time to get dinner, he would have noticed it? By eight o'clock it became obvious that she must have told him she would not be back in time for dinner. No doubt she had told him about the ham loaf, too. She was thoughtful about such matters—which was one reason why her conversation was so seldom arresting. It would not do to seem inattentive, so he would eat and, if there was time before she got back, he would also wash up.

He ate. He washed up. He hung the dishcloth on the rail. In some ways he was a born bachelor.

The telephone rang. As he expected, it was Golding, who had said he might come round that evening with the stamp album he had inherited from an uncle who had gone in for philately. He didn't know if there was anything in it worth having; Ridpath would know. Golding was one of those calm, tractable bores who appear to have been left over from ampler days. Every Sunday he walked from Earls Court to St. Paul's to attend matins. Now he arrived carrying a large brown-paper parcel and a bunch of violets. "Lucy's out," said Aston, seeing Golding look round for somewhere to dispose of the flowers. "She's gone out to dinner. Have a whisky?"

"Well, yes. That would be very pleasant."

The album turned out to be unexpectedly interesting. It was after eleven when Golding began to wrap it up. His eye fell on the violets.

"I don't suppose I shall see Mrs. Ridpath. I think you said she was dining out."

"She's dining with some friends."

"Rather a long dinner," said Golding.

"You know what women are like when they get together," said Aston. "Talk, talk, talk."

Golding said sympathetically, "Well, I like talking, too."

Golding was gone. As Aston picked up his violets, which would have to be put into some sort of vase, he realized with painful actuality that if Lucy wasn't back by midnight he would have to do something about it—ring up hospitals, ring up the police. It would be necessary to describe her. When one has been happily married to a woman for nearly twenty-five years it is too much to be expected to describe her. Tall. Thin. Knock-kneed. Walks with a stoop. Brown eyes, brown hair—probably safer to say grizzled. Wearing— How the hell was he to know what Lucy would be wearing if she had gone out to dinner? If he were to say what occurred to him, it would be tweeds.

Suppose she had not gone out to dinner? Suppose—for fiction is after all based on real life—suppose she had gone off, leaving that traditional note on her pincushion? If she had a pincushion. He walked into their bedroom. There was a pincushion, a very old and wilted one, but there was no note on it. He could see no note anywhere. There were some letters on her desk. He read them. They were from shops, or from friends, recounting what the friends had been doing.

If only he had listened! If only she had not got into this unfortunate trick of mumbling! For she would certainly have told him whom she was going out to. "Aston, I'm having dinner with . . ." It seemed as if he could almost recapture the words. "Aston, I'm going . . ." Could she have continued, "away for the weekend"? For that would explain everything. It was perfectly possible. There were all those friends who wrote to her about flying in Hovercrafts to the Isle of Wight, visiting Leningrad, coming back from cruises to the West Indies. Why shouldn't she be spending the weekend with one or other of these Sibyls or Sophies? It was April, a season when it is natural to spend weekends in the country—if you like that sort of thing. Only a few weeks ago he had remarked that she was looking tired and would be the better for country air. An invitation had come; mindful of his encouragement she had accepted it. He could now almost swear he had heard the words "Aston, I am going away for the weekend." No doubt she had also told him where. He had failed to remember it, but one cannot remember everything.

He ate some biscuits, went to bed with a clear conscience, and was asleep in five minutes.

In the morning his first conscious thought was that Lucy was away for the weekend. The conviction was so strong that presently he was able to imagine her being brought breakfast in bed—brown-bread toast, honey, piping-hot coffee; he could positively see the tray. There she would lie, listening to the birds. If it had not been for that unlucky moment of inattention, he would have been able to construct some approximation of the surrounding landscape. London is surrounded by the Home Counties. Somewhere in the Home Counties—for if she had told him she was going to Yorkshire or Cape Wrath he would surely have registered the fact—Lucy was having breakfast in bed. He was glad of it. It would do her good. Thinking affectionately of Lucy, he lay in bed for some while longer, then got up and made his breakfast. The bacon took a long time to cook. He had omitted to riddle the stove overnight; the fire had choked and was almost out. He looked about conscientiously to see if Lucy had left any food he ought to heat up. He did not want to be found with any kind provisions uneaten. When Lucy went to visit her cousin Aurelia in Suffolk, she always left, he remembered, quantities of soup. This time she had left nothing. No doubt she had said, at that moment when he wasn't attending, that he had better eat out.

Accordingly, Aston ate out. His mind was at rest. Wherever Lucy might be, she could not be with Aurelia and would return from wherever it might have been his own normal Lucy. During those Suffolk absences all he could be sure of was that Aurelia was leading Lucy, whether up a windmill or to Paris, by the nose, and that what he received back would be Aurelia's Lucy: talking in Aurelia's voice, asserting Aurelia's opinions, aping Aurelia's flightiness, flushed, overexcited, and giggling like a schoolgirl. Thoroughly unsettled, in short, and needing several days to become herself again. Family affection is all very well, but it was absurd that visits to a country cousin—a withered virgin and impecunious at that—should be so intoxicating that Lucy returned from them as from an assignation, and acknowledged them as such by leaving him with such quantities of soup. Even when she went to Aurelia's funeral she provided it; and came home saying in Aurelia's voice that cremations would be all right if they weren't so respectful. But now there was no soup and his mind continued to be at rest till he was in the bathroom brushing his teeth before going to bed and noticed Lucy's sponge. It was a new sponge; he had given it to her for Christmas. There was no excuse for leaving it behind. Apparently she had not taken anything—not her hand lotion, not her dusting powder. Examining Lucy's dressing table, he saw that she had taken nothing from that, either. In a moment of blind panic he fell on his knees and looked for her body under the bed.

This was probably due to Wordsworth's tiresome trick of staying about in one's memory. If Lucy had been christened Angelina, he would not have been under the same compulsion to suppose she was dead. Lucy (his Lucy) kept Wordsworth beside her bed. He looked up the poem and found that on this occasion Wordsworth was mistaken, though in the following lyrics he had lost her and it made a great difference to him. Then he remembered that Samuel Butler had wickedly put it about that Wordsworth, aided by Southey and Coleridge, had murdered Lucy. This meant returning to the sitting room for Butler. Half an hour with Butler recalled him to reason. Lucy must have forgotten to pack her sponge and had bought a new hairbrush.

But the sponge and the hairbrush had shaken him. He did not sleep so well that night, and when he got up to a cold, companionless Monday morning the reality of Lucy's absence was stronger than the ideality of her breakfast tray floating somewhere in the Home Counties, and he hoped very much she would soon be back—by which time Mrs. Barker would have put things straight, so that there would be nothing to impede him from saying, "And now tell me all about it." For that was the form of words he had decided on.

When he came back that evening everything had been put straight. But still there was no Lucy.

Anxiety hardens the heart. Addressing the absent Lucy, Aston said, "I shall ring up Vere." Vere was his sister—a successful widow. He did not like her very much and Lucy did not like her at all. She lived in Hampstead. He rang up Vere, who cut short his explanations by saying she would come at once and grapple.

She came with a suitcase and again cut short his explanations.

"I suppose you have told the police."

"Told the police, Vere? Why the hell should I tell the police? It's no business of theirs. Nothing would induce me to tell the police."

"If Lucy doesn't reappear and you haven't told the police, you'll probably be suspected of murder."

As Aurelia walked toward the Tate Gallery she noticed that she was wearing a wedding ring. Her first impulse—for she was a flighty creature—was to drop it into a pillar-box. Then some streak of latent prudence persuaded her that it would be more practical to sell it. She pulled it off—it was too large for her and revolved easily on her finger—and dropped it into her bag. She remembered that there had been a second-hand jewelry shop a little farther along. She had sometimes looked in through its wire-meshed windows at coral earrings and mosaic brooches of the Colosseum, St. Peter's, and other large celebrities. Once, long ago, she had bought herself an unset moss agate there. It was only a simulacrum of moss, but the best that then presented itself. The shop was still in its old place. She went in and presented the ring. The jeweler looked with compassion at the sad middle-aged woman in a mackintosh with a wisp of graying hair plastered to her forehead by the rain. To judge by the ring, she must have known better days. It was both broad and heavy, and he could give her a good sum for it. "I'm afraid I must ask for the name," he said. "It's a formality."

"Aurelia Lefanu, Shilling Street, Lavenham." She smiled as she gave the address.

Well, at any rate, the poor thing loved her home.

The same unaccountable streak of prudence now told Aurelia she must do some shopping. Stockings, for instance. It was raining harder, and her feet felt wet already. One need suggested another, and impressed by her own efficiency she bought some underclothes. Finally, as it was now raining extremely hard and she had collected several paper parcels, she bought a tartan grip. The Tate would be full of people who had gone in to shelter from the rain; but they wouldn't be looking at the Turners. Joseph Mallord William Turner, staring from under his sooty chimney-pot hat, sucking in color as if from a fruit, making and remaking his world like some unendingly ambitious Jehovah and, like a Jehovah, peopling it with rather unsuccessful specimens of the human race, was hers and hers alone for the next hour. When she left the gallery, Joseph Mallord William Turner had got there before her. The rain had stopped. A glittering light thrust from beneath the arch of cloud and painted the river with slashing strokes of primrose and violet. The tide was at the full, and a procession of Thames shipping rode on it in blackness and majesty.

"Oh!"

In her excitement she seized the elbow of the man beside her; for he too was looking, he too, no doubt, was transfixed. Touched by her extreme emotion and her extreme wetness, he said, "I'm hoping to catch a taxi. Can I give you a lift? It's going to pelt again in a moment, you know."

"I've forgotten to take out my bag. Could you wait an instant?"

Seeing its cheapness—indeed, he could read the price, for the tag was still hanging from it—he supposed she was some perpetual student who would be the better for a good square tea. She had a pretty voice.

The light grew dazzling. In another minute a heavier rain would descend; if he could not secure the taxi that had just drawn up to discharge its passenger, there would be no hope of another. He hauled her down the steps, signaling with her tartan bag, and pushed her in.

"Where can I take you?"

"Where? . . . I really don't know. Where would be suitable?" And gazing out of the window at the last defiance of the light, she murmured, " 'Whither will I not go with gentle Ithamore?' "

He gave his own address to the driver. The taxi drove off.

Turning to him, she said, "Marlowe, not me. I'm afraid it may have sounded rather forward."

"I've never been called Ithamore in all my life. It's a pretty name. What's yours?"

"Mine's a pretty name, too. Aurelia."

So it was in London that she breakfasted in bed, that Sunday morning, wearing white silk pajamas with black froggings— for however cleverly one goes shopping one cannot remember everything, and she had forgotten to buy a nightdress. In all his life he had never been called Ithamore. In all his life he had never met anything like Aurelia. She was middle-aged, plain, badly kept, untraveled—and she had the aplomb of a *poule de luxe.* Till quite recently she must have worn a wedding ring, for the dent was on her finger; but she bore no other mark of matrimony. She knew how to look at pictures, and from her ease in nakedness he might have supposed her a model—but her movements never set into a pose. He could only account for her by supposing she had escaped from a lunatic asylum.

She must be saved from any more of that. He must get her out of England as soon as possible. This would involve getting him out of England, too, which would be inconvenient for Jerome and Marmor, Art Publishers, but the firm could survive his absence for a few weeks. It would not be longer than that. Once settled at Saint-Rémy de Provence, with Laure and Dominique to keep an eye on her, and with a polite subsidy, she would do very well for herself—set up an easel, maybe; study astronomy. She would feel no need for him. It was he who would feel need, be consumed with an expert's curiosity.

She had spoken of how Cézanne painted trees in slats, so he drove her through the beechwoods round Stokenchurch and along a canal to a hotel that concealed its very good cooking behind a rustic Edwardian face. Here she said she was tired of eating cooked food, she would prefer fruit. She was as frank as a nymph about it, or a kinkajou. This frankness was part of her savor. It touched him because it was so totally devoid of calculation or self-consciousness. It would have been remarkable even in a very young girl; in a middle-aged woman showing such marks of wear and tear it was resplendent. It was touching, too, though rather difficult to take, that she should be so unappreciative of his tact. He had led her to a prospect of Provence; he had intimated that he sometimes went there himself; that he might have to go there quite soon; that he hoped it might be almost immediately, in order to catch the nightingales and the wisteria. . . .

"Will you take me, too?" she inquired. To keep his feet on the ground, he asked if she had a passport.

On Monday morning he rang up Jerome and Marmor to say he had a cold and would not be coming in for a few days; and would Miss Simpson bring him a passport-application form, please. The form was brought. He left Aurelia to fill it in while he went to his bank. As this was a first application, someone would have to vouch for her, and he would ask Dawkins to do it. Dawkins was closeted with a customer. He had to wait. When he got at him, Dawkins was so concerned to show that the slight illegality of vouching for someone he had never set eyes on meant nothing to him that he launched into conversation and told funny stories about Treasury officials for the next fifteen minutes.

"Aurelia! I'm sorry to have left you for so long. . . . Aurelia?"

Standing in the emptied room he continued to say, "Aurelia." The application form lay on the table. With a feeling of indecency, he read it. "AURELIA LEFANU. Born: Burford, Oxon. 11th May 1923. Height: 5 ft. 10. Eyes: Brown. Hair: Gray." The neat printing persisted without a waver. But at the Signature of Applicant something must have happened. She had begun to write—it seemed to be a name beginning with "L"—and had violently, scrawlingly erased it.

She had packed her miserable few belongings and was gone. For several weeks he haunted the Tate Gallery and waited to read an unimportant paragraph saying that the body of a woman, aged about forty-five, had been recovered from the Thames.

"If you haven't told the police—" The thought of being suspected of murdering Lucy left Aston speechless. The aspersion was outrageous; the notion was ridiculous. Twenty years and more had passed since they were on murdering terms. But the police were capable of believing anything, and Vere's anxiety to establish his innocence was already a rope round his neck. Vere was at the telephone, saying that Mr. Ridpath wished to see an officer immediately. There appeared to be some demurring at the other end, but she overcame it. While they waited, she filled in the time by cross-examining him. When did Lucy tell him she was going away for the weekend? How did she look when telling him? If he wasn't quite sure that she had done so, what made him think she had? Had she been going away for other weekends? Had he noticed any change in her? Was she restless at night? Flushed? Hysterical? Had her speech thickened? If not, why did he say she mumbled? Had he looked in all her drawers? Her wardrobe? The wastepaper baskets? Why not? Had she drawn out money from her post-office savings? Had she been growing morbid? Had she been buying cosmetics, new clothes, neglecting the house, reading poetry, losing her temper? Why hadn't he noticed any of this? Were they growing apart? Did she talk in her sleep? Why did she never come to Hampstead? And why had he waited till Monday evening before saying a word of all this?

When the police officer came, she transferred the cross-examination to him. He was a large, calm man in need of sleep, and resolutely addressed himself to Aston. Aston began to feel better.

"And you were the last person to see Mrs. Ridpath?"

Interrupting Vere's florid confirmation, Aston had the pleasure of saying "No," and the further pleasure of saving her face. "My sister has forgotten about our charwoman. Mrs. Barker must have seen her after I did. She came up in the lift just as I was leaving for work."

The police officer made a note of Mrs. Barker and went away, saying that every endeavor would be made. "But if the lady should be suffering from a loss of memory, it may not be so easy to find her."

"Why?" said Vere. "I should have thought—"

"When persons lose their memory, in a manner of speaking they lose themselves. They aren't themselves. It would surprise you how unrecognizable they become."

When he had gone, Vere exclaimed, "Stuff and nonsense! I'm sure I could recognize Lucy a mile off. And she hasn't much to be recognized by, except her stoop."

Bereft of male companionship, Aston sat down with his head in his hands. Vere began to unpack.

She was in the kitchen, routing through the store-cupboard, when Mrs. Barker arrived on Tuesday morning. She said, "Well, I suppose you know about Mrs. Ridpath?"

Mrs. Barker put down her bag, took off her hat and coat, opened the bag, drew out an apron and tied it on. Then, folding her hands on her stomach, she replied, "No, Madam. Not that I know of." Her heart sank; but a strong dislike is a strong support.

"Well, she's gone. And Mr. Ridpath has put it in the hands of the police."

"Indeed, Madam."

"Not that that will be much use. You know what the police are like."

"No, Madam. I have had no dealings with them."

"They bungle everything. Now, why three packets of prunes? It does seem extraordinary. She was the last person in the world one would expect to do anything unexpected. Did she ever talk to you about going away? By herself, I mean?"

"No, Madam. Never."

Mrs. Barker had no doubt as to where Lucy had gone. She had gone to the South of France—to a pale landscape full of cemetery trees, as in the picture postcard, not sent by anyone, which she kept stuck in her dressing glass and said was the South of France. Remarking that she must get on with her work, Mrs. Barker went smoothly to the bedroom, removed the postcard, and tucked it into her bosom.

Loath as she was to admit that her sister-in-law could have a lover, Vere was sure that she had eloped. (Men are so helpless, their feelings so easily played on.) She was sure that Lucy's detestable charwoman knew her whereabouts and had been heavily bribed. A joint elevenses was when she'd catch the woman and trip her into the truth.

This was forestalled by Mrs. Barker bringing her a tray for

one at ten-fifty, remarking that Madam might be glad of it,
seeing how busy she was with her writing; and quitting the
room with an aggressively hushed tread. Vere believed in leaving no stone unturned. Though she was sure that Lucy had
eloped, this didn't seem to have occurred to Aston yet. A series
of confidential letters to Lucy's friends might produce evi-
dence that would calm his mind. Not one of the tiresome
women had signed with more than a given name, so the enve-
lopes would have to be directed to "Sibyl," "Sophie," "Peg,"
and "Lalla;" but a "Dear Madam" would redress that. The
rest would be easy: a preliminary announcement that she was
Aston's sister and was writing to say that Lucy had left home
for no apparent reason since she and Aston had always seemed
such a happy couple; and that if Lalla, Peg, Sophie, or Sibyl
could throw any light on this, of course in strictest confidence,
it would be an inexpressible relief. More she would not say;
she did not want to prejudice anyone against Lucy.

All this took time. The friends might know each other and
get together; it would not do if her letters to them were iden-
tical. It would suggest a circular. Her four letters done—for
she did not propose to write to people like the linendraper in
Northern Ireland who regretted he could no longer supply
huckaback roller towels—she would get to work on Mrs. Barker; differently, this time, and appealing to her feelings.

It was in vain. However, she managed to get the woman's
address from her, so she rang up the police station and stated
her conviction that Mrs. Barker knew what she wouldn't say
and should be questioned and, if need be, watched. As Vere
was one of those people who are obeyed—on the fallacious hypothesis that it tends to keep them quiet—an inspector called
that afternoon on Mrs. Barker. He could not have been pleas-
anter, but the harm had been done; everybody in the street
would know she had been visited by the police. Both the children knew it when they got in—David from school, Diane

from her job at the fruiterer's. "Mum! Whatever's happened?"
"Mum! Is anything wrong?"

The sight of them turned the sword in her heart. But she
did not waver. Go back to those Ridpaths she would not; nor
demean herself by asking for the money she was owed, though
it might mean that the payments on David's bicycle and the
triple mirror in Diane's bedroom could not be kept up. Pinch,
pawn, go on the streets or the Public Assistance—but grovel
for her lawful money to that two-faced crocodile who set the
police on her she would not. She drew on her savings; and
comforted herself with the thought of the two-faced crocodile
down on her knees and doing her own scrubbing. The picture
was visionary. Vere was on a committee—among other
committees—of a Training Home for Endangered Girls, and
whistled up an endangered mental deficient in no time.

"Now, now," Aurelia abjured herself, gathering her belongings
together. "Now, now. Quickly does it. Don't lose your head."
Going down in the lift she was accompanied by the man in
Dante—the decapitated man who held his head in front of
him like a lantern and said through its lips, "Woe's me." But
fortunately he got stuck in the swing door. She was alone in
the street and knew that she must find a bus. A taxi would
not do, it must be a bus; for a bus asks you nothing, it substi-
tutes its speed and direction for yours, it takes you away from
your private life. You sit in it, released, unknown, an anonymous destiny, and look out of the window or read the adver-
tisements. A bus that had gone by at speed slowed as a van
came out of a side street. She ran, caught up with it just as it
moved again, clambered in, and sat down next to a stout man
who said to her, "You had to run for it, my girl." She smiled,
too breathless to speak., Her smile betrayed her. He saw she
was not so young as he took her for. She spent the day traveling about London in buses, with a bun now and then to keep

her strength up. In the evening she attended a free lecture on town and country planning, given under the auspices of the London County Council. This was in Clerkenwell. During the lecture she noticed that her hands had left off shaking and that for a second time she had yawned quite naturally. Whatever it had been she had so desperately escaped from, she had escaped it. Like the lecture, she was free. It had been rather an expensive day. She atoned for this by walking to King's Cross and spending the night in the ladies' waiting room. It was warm, lofty, impartial—preferable, really, to any bedroom. The dutiful trains arrived and departed—demonstrations of a world in which all was controlled and orderly and would get on very nicely without her. Tomorrow she would go to some quiet place—Highgate Cemetery would do admirably—and decide where to go next.

It was in Highgate Cemetery, studying a headstone which said "I will dwell in the house of the Lord for ever," that Aurelia remembered hostels. The lecturer in Clerkenwell had enlarged on youth hostels. But there were middle-aged hostels, too—quiet establishments, scenes of unlicensed sobriety; and as youth hostels are scattered in wild landscapes for the active who enjoyed rock-climbing and rambling (he had dwelt on rambling and the provision of ramblers' routes), middle-aged hostels are clustered round devotional landmarks for the sedentary who enjoyed going to compline. She had enough money to dwell in a middle-aged hostel for a week. A week was quite far enough to plan for. Probably the best person to consult would be a clergyman. There was bound to be a funeral before long. She would hang on its outskirts and buttonhole the man afterward. "Excuse me," she would begin. "I am a stranger. . . ."

"Excuse me," she began, laying hold of him by the surplice. He had a sad, unappreciated face. "I am a stranger."

Thinking about her afterward—and she was to haunt his mind for the rest of his life—Lancelot Fogg acknowledged a saving mercy. His Maker, whom he had come to despair of, an ear that never heard, a name that he was incessantly obliged to take in vain, had done a marvel and shown him a spiritual woman. His life was full of women: good women, pious women, energetic, forceful women, blighted women, women abounding in good works, women learned in liturgies, women with tragedies, scruples, fallen arches—not to mention women he was compelled to classify as bad women: bullies, slanderers, backbiters, schemers, organizers, women abounding in wrath; there were even a few kind women. But never a spiritual woman till now. So tall and so thin, so innocently frank, it was as if she had come down from the west front of Chartres into a world where she was a stranger.

There was nothing remarkable in what she had to say. She wanted to find a hostel somewhere away from London—but not far, because of paying for the ticket—where she could be quiet and go to compline and do some washing. He understood about washing, for being poor he sometimes tried to do his own. But her spirituality shone through her words; it was as if a lily were speaking of cleanliness. Spirituality shone even more clearly through her silences. While he was searching his mind for addresses, she looked at him with tranquil interest, unconcerned trust, as though she had never in her life known care or frustration—whereas from the lines in her face it was obvious she had known both. She was so exceedingly tranquil and trustful, in fact, that she gave an impression of impermanence—as if at any moment some bidding might twitch her away. Nonattachment, he remembered, was the word. The spiritual become nonattached.

"Would Bedfordshire be too far?"

"I don't think so. I should only be there a week."

He had remembered one of the women in his life who had been kind and who now kept a guesthouse near a Benedictine monastery. He gave her the address. She thanked him and was gone. So was the funeral party. The grave was being filled in with increasing briskness. That afternoon, he must preside at the quarterly meeting of St. Agatha's Guild.

The mistake, thought Aurelia, had been to dwell on compline. Doing so she had given a false impression of herself. The recommended Miss Larke of St. Hilda's Guesthouse had no sooner let her in than she was exclaiming, "Just in time, just in time! Reverend Fogg rang up to say you were coming—the silly man forgot to mention your name, but you are the lady he met, aren't you?—and that you would be going to compline. I'm afraid we've finished supper. But I'll keep some soup hot for you for when you get back. And here is Mrs. Bouverie who will show you the way. She's waited on purpose."

"How do you do? How kind of you. My name is Lefanu. Is the abbey far away?"

"If we start now we'll make it," said Mrs. Bouverie.

They started. Mrs. Bouverie was short and stout and she had a short stout manner of speech. Presently she inquired, "R.C. or A.C.?"

Aurelia was at a loss. The question suggested electricity or taps.

"Roman or Anglo?"

Aurelia replied, "Anglo." It seemed safer, though it was difficult to be sure in the dark.

"Mrs. or Miss?"

Aurelia replied, "Miss."

She had felt so sure that she would be fed on arrival that this day, too, she had relied on buns, resisting those jellied eels which looked so interesting in the narrow street that twisted down to the river—for instead of going straight to the guesthouse she had spent an hour or so exploring the town to see if she'd like it. She did like it. But she had never eaten jellied eels.

She had never been to compline, either. This made it impossible to guess how long it would go on, or exactly what was going on, except that people were invisibly singing or reciting in leisured tones. If she had not been so hungry, Aurelia decided, she could have understood why compline should exercise this charm on people. There was a total lack of obligation about it which was very agreeable. And when it had mysteriously become over, and they were walking back, and Mrs. Bouverie remarked how beautifully it ended a day, didn't it, Aurelia agreed—while looking forward to the soup. The soup was lentil. It was hot and thick, and she felt her being fasten on it. The room was full of chairs, the chairs were full of people, the television was on. She sat clasping the mug where the soup had been. But it wilted in her grasp. She knew that at all costs she must not faint. "Smelling salts!" she exclaimed. A flask of vinegar was pressed to her nose, her head was bowed between her knees. When she had been taken off to be put to bed with a hot-water bottle, Mrs. Bouverie announced, "She's Anglo."

"Naturally. They are always so absurdly emotional," said a lady who was Roman.

Miss Larke returned, reporting that the poor thing was touchingly grateful and had forgotten to bring a nightdress.

In the morning Aurelia woke hungry but without a vestige of gratitude. The sun shone, a thrush was singing in the garden, it was a perfect drying day.

Aurelia, the replacement of Lucy, was a nova—a new appearance in the firmament, the explosion of an aging star. A nova is seen where no star was and is seen as a portent, a promise of what is variously desired: a victory, a pestilence, the birth of a hero, a rise in the price of corn. To the man never before called Ithamore she was at last an object of art he could not account for. To Lancelot Fogg she was at last a spiritual woman. To the denizens of St. Hilda's guesthouse she was something new to talk about—arresting but harmless. At least, she was harmless till the evening she brought in that wretched tomcat and insisted on keeping it as a pet. If Lancelot Fogg had not recommended her so fervently, Aurelia with that misnamed pet of hers would have been directed to lodgings elsewhere. It was bad enough to adopt a most unhealthy-looking tomcat, but to call the animal Lucy made it so much worse; it seemed a deliberate flout, a device to call attention to the creature's already too obvious sex.

"But why Lucy, Miss Lefanu? Surely it's inappropriate?"

"It's a family name," she replied.

Lucy developed on Aurelia's fourth evening at the guest-house. She was again accompanying Mrs. Bouverie to compline when a distant braying caught her ear. Looking in the direction of the braying, she saw a livid glow and exclaimed, "A circus!"

"It's that dreadful fair," Mrs. Bouverie replied. "As I was telling you, my brother-in-law who had that delightful place in Hampshire, not far from Basinstoke, such rhododendrons! I've never seen such a blaze of color as when they were out. . . ."

When she had seen Mrs. Bouverie safely down on her knees, Aurelia stole away and went off to find the fair. Fairs, of course, are not what they used to be, but they are still what they are, and Aurelia enjoyed herself a great deal till two haunted young men in frock coats and ringlets attached themselves to her, saying at intervals, "Spare us a reefer, beautiful. Have a heart." For they, too, had seen her as a nova. At last she managed to give them the slip and hurried away through the loud entrails of a Lunar Flight. This brought her to the outskirts of the fair, and it was there she saw the cat lying on the muddied grass under the bonnet of a lorry. Its eyes were shut, its ears laid back. It had gone under the lorry bonnet for warmth, and was paying the price.

When she came back with a hot dog, it had rearranged itself. In its new attitude she could see how thin it was and how despairingly shabby. She knelt down and addressed it from a distance. It heard her, for it turned its head away. The smell of the hot dog was more persuasive. It began to thresh its tail.

"You'll eat when I'm gone," she said, with fellow-feeling, and scattered bits of hot dog under the bonnet and began to walk away—knowing that its precarious balance between mistrust and self-preservation could be overset by a glance. She had left the fairground and was turning into a street full of warehouses when she saw that the cat, limping and cringing, was following her. She stopped, and it came on till it was beside her. Then it sat down and raised its face toward her. Its expression was completely mute—and familiar. The cat was exactly like her cousin Lucy.

When she picked it up it relaxed in her arms, rubbed its head against her shoulder, and purred. The cat took it absolutely for granted that it should be carried off by a deity. Still throned in her arms, it blinked serenely at the mortals in the guesthouse, sure that they soon would be disposed of.

There were a great many things to be done for Lucy. His suppurating paw had to be dressed, his ears had to be cleaned and his coat brushed, food had to be bought for him, and four times a day he had to be exercised in the garden. In the intervals of this, his fleas had to be dealt with. Using a fine-tooth comb she searched them out, pounced on them, dropped them in a bowl of soapy water, resumed the search. It was a dreamlike occupation: it put her in touch with the infinite. Twenty. Thirty. Forty-seven. Fifty-two. From time to time she looked sharply at the bowl of soapy water and pushed back any wretches that had struggled to the rim.

The total of fleas went up in bounds. The money in her purse decreased. Even using the utmost economy, stealing whenever she conveniently could, having sardines put down to Miss Larke, she would not be left with enough to pay for a second week at the guesthouse. Lucy's paw healed slowly; it would be some while yet before he could provide for himself. She noticed that Lucy's paw was increasingly asked about; that suggestions for his welfare multiplied.

"I wonder why you don't put an advertisement in the local

paper, saying 'Found.' All this time his real owners may be hunting for him, longing to get him back."

Aurelia looked deeply at the speaker. It might be worth trying. There is no harm in blackmail, since no one is obliged to give in to it. On the other hand, it is no good unless they do.

She composed two letters: "Unless you send me fifty pounds in notes, I shan't be able to come back." "Unless you send me fifty pounds in notes, I shall be forced to return."

Combing out fleas to a new rhythm of "he loves me, he loves me not," she weighed these alternatives. The second would probably have the stronger appeal to Aston's heart. Poor Aston, she had defrauded him too long of the calm expansion of widowerhood. But the stomach is a practical organ; the first alternative might be the more compelling. She did not, of course, mean to return, in either case. Since her adoption of Lucy, she had become so unshakably Aurelia that she could contemplate being Lucy, too, so far as being Lucy would further Aurelia's designs. But Lucy, the former Lucy, must be Aurelia's property. There must be no little escapades into identity, no endorsing of checks, no more slidings into Lucy Ridpath. That was why the money must come in notes. Even so, who was it to be addressed to?

It was time for Lucy to scratch in the garden. For the first time, he tried to scratch with both hind legs. Everything became easy. Whichever the chosen form of the letter demanding money with menaces, Aurelia, signing with a capital L., would ask for the money to be directed to Miss Lefanu, *poste restante.* Lucy had been Lefanu when Aston married her. He could not have forgotten this; it might even touch his heart and dispose him to add another five pounds. All that remained was to decide which letter to send, and to post it from Bedford, which was nearby and noncommittal. The envelope had been posted before she realized that both letters were enclosed.

"Lucy's handwriting," said Aston. "She's alive. What an infinite relief!"

"I never supposed she wasn't," said Vere. "Still, if it's a relief to you to see her handwriting—it doesn't seem such a niggle as usual, but that's her 'R'—I'm sure I'm glad."

"But Vere, on Monday evening, on *Monday evening,* you said I must ring up the police or I should be suspected of murdering her."

"So you would have been. They always jump to conclusions. Well, what does Lucy say?" The letters had been folded up together. The first alternative was uppermost.

"She seems to have got into some sort of trouble. She says she can't come home unless I send her fifty pounds."

"Fifty pounds? Where is she, then. California?"

"The postmark is Bedford. She's gone back to her maiden name."

"Fifty pounds to get back from Bedford. Fifty pounds! She must have got herself mixed up in something pretty fishy. Yes. I heard only the other day that Bedford is an absolute hotbed of the drug traffic. That's what she wants the money for. Poor silly Lucy, she'd be wax in their hands. Aston! You'll have to think very carefully, apart from this absurd demand for money, about having her back. If she were here alone all day with no one to keep an eye on her— What does she say on the second sheet?"

"Is there a second sheet? I hadn't noticed. She says— Vere, I can't make this out. She says, 'Unless you send me fifty pounds in notes I shall be forced to return.'"

"Nonsense, Aston! You're misreading it. She just made a fair copy and then put them both in."

"But Vere, she says unless I send her the money she will be forced to return."

"She must be raving. Why on earth should she expect you to pay her to keep away? Let me see."

After a pause, she said, "My poor Aston."

Her voice was heavy with commiseration. It fell on Aston like a wet sponge. His brief guilty dazzle of relief (for provided Lucy wasn't dead he really didn't want to live with her again; what he wanted was manly solitude, and he had already taken the first steps toward getting shot of Vere) sizzled out.

"Poor Lucy! I must send her something, I suppose."

"Yes, you ought to. But not too much. Ten pounds would be ample. What's Bedford? No way at all."

When Aurelia called at the post office, the clerk handed her two letters. She opened Aston's first.

> Dear Lucy,
>
> I will not try to persuade you. The heart has its reasons. But if a time ever comes when you want to come back, remember there will always be a door on the latch and a light in the window.
>
> I will say nothing of the anxiety your leaving without a word has caused me.
>
> —Aston

Four five-pound notes were enclosed.

The other letter was from Vere. It ran:

> Aston is now recovering. I will thankfully pay you to keep away.

This letter was accompanied by ten ten-pound notes.

Aurelia bought Lucy some tinned salmon and a handsome traveling basket. But for the greater part of that afternoon's journey, Lucy sat erect on her knee looking out of the window and held like a diviner's twig by his two front legs. She relied on Lucy to know at a snuff which station to get out at, just as he had known how to succeed in blackmailing—for while she was debating which of the two letters to send he had leaped onto the table, laid his head on her hand, and rolled with such ardor and abandonment that she forgot all else, so both letters went off in the one envelope. Relying on Lucy, she had chosen a stopping train. It joggled through a green unemphatic landscape with many willow trees and an occasional broached spire. Lucy remained unmoved. She began to wonder if his tastes ran to the romantic, if high mountains were to him a feeling—in which case she had brought him to quite the wrong part of England. In the opposite corner sat a man with leather patches on his elbows, paying them no attention. Then at a station called Peckover Junction two ladies got in, and resumed (they were traveling together) a conversation about their grandchildren. From their grandchildren they turned to the ruin of the countryside—new towns, overspill, and holiday camps.

"Look at those caravans! They've got here, now."

"Don't speak to me of caravans," said the other lady.

Disregarding this, the first lady asked if there were as many as ever.

"More! Such hideosities at poor Betcombe . . . and the children! Swarming everywhere. I shall never find a tenant now. Besides, all these new people have such grand ideas. They must have this, they must have that. They don't appreciate the past. For me, that's its charm. If it weren't for the caravans, I'd be at Betcombe still, glorying in my beams and my pump. Do you know, it was eighteenth century, my pump?"

"Would you like me as a tenant?" said Aurelia. "I can't give you any references just now, but I'd pay ten shillings a week. No, darling!" This last remark was addressed to Lucy, who had driven his claws into her thigh.

"Ten shillings a week—for my lovely little cottage?"

"A pound a week."

"Really, this is so sudden, so unusual. No references . . . and I suppose you'd be bringing that cat. I'm a bird-lover. No, I'm afraid it's out of the question. Come, Mary, we get out here."

For the train was coming to a halt. Both ladies gathered

their belongings and got out. From the window Aurelia saw them get in again, a few carriages farther up.

"You're well out of that," observed the man with leather patches. "I know her place. It'a a hovel. No room to swing a cat in, begging your cat's pardon."

Lucy rounded himself like a poultice above his scratch. Aurelia said she expected she had been silly. The train went on. An atmosphere of acquaintance established itself. Presently the man asked if she had any particular place in mind.

"No. Not exactly. I'm a stranger."

"Because I happen to know of something that might suit you—if you don't object to it being a bit out of the way. It's a bungalow, and it's modern. If you're agreeable, I'll take you to see it."

It was impossible not to be agreeable, because he was so plainly a shy man and surprised at finding himself intervening. So when he got out she got out with him, and he took her to a Railway Arms where she and Lucy would be comfortable, and said he would call for her at ten the next morning.

He was exactly punctual. When she had assured him how comfortable she and Lucy had been, there seemed to be nothing more to say. Fortunately, he was one of those drivers who give their whole mind to driving. They drove in his van. It was lettered "George Bastable, Builder and Plumber," and among the things in the back was a bathtub wrapped in cellophane. They drove eastward, through the same uneventful landscape. He turned the van into a track that ran uphill— only slightly uphill, but in that flat landscape it seemed considerable. "There it is."

A spinney of mixed trees ran along the top of the ridge. Smoke was rising through the boughs. So she would have a neighbor. She had not reckoned on that.

But the smoke was rising from the chimney of a bungalow, and there was no other building there.

He must have got up very early, for the fire was well established, the room was warm and felt inhabited. The kitchen floor was newly washed and a newspaper path was spread across it.

"You'd find it comfortable," he said.

"Oh, yes," she said, looking at the two massive armchairs that faced each other across a hideous hearth mat.

"It hasn't been lived in for three years, though I come out from time to time to give a look to it. But no damp anywhere —that'll show how sound it is."

"No. It feels wonderfully dry," she said, looking at a flight of blue pottery birds on the wall.

Lucy was shaking his basket.

"May I let your cat out? He'd like a run, and I daresay he'd pick up a breakfast, bird's-nesting."

Before she could answer, he had unfastened the lid and Lucy had bounded over the threshold. How was she to answer this man who had taken so much trouble and was so proud of his bungalow?

"Did you build it yourself?"

"I did. That's why I know it's a good one. I built it for my young lady. When I saw you in the train, you put me in mind of her, somehow. So when you said you wanted somewhere to live—" He stared at her, standing politely at a distance, trying to recapture the appearance of his nova in this halfhearted lady, no longer young.

The house had stood empty for three years. She had died. Poor Mr. Bastable! Aurelia's face assumed the right expression.

"She left," he said.

"How *could* she?" exclaimed Aurelia.

This time, there was no need to put on the right expression. She was wholeheartedly shocked at the behavior of Mr. Bastable's young lady—and if the young lady had come in just then she would have boxed the ungrateful minx's ears. Instead, it was Lucy who trotted in, looking smug, with fragments of eggshell plastered to his chops, sat down in front of the fire, and began cleaning himself. Mr. Bastable remarked that Lucy had found a robin's nest. He was grateful for Aurelia's indignation but shy of saying so. He suspected he had gone too far. Somewhat to his surprise he learned that Aurelia would like to move into his lovely bungalow immediately. He drove her to the village to do her shopping, came back to show her where the coal was kept, gave her the key. Watching him drive away she suddenly became aware of the landscape she would soon be taking for granted. It sparkled with crisscrossing drains and ditches; a river wound through it. A herd of caravans was peacefully grazing in the distance.

Happiness is an immunity. In a matter of days Aurelia was unaffected by the flight of blue pottery birds, sat in armchairs so massive she could not move them and felt no wish to move them, slept deliciously between pink nylon sheets. With immunity she watched Lucy sharpening his claws on the massive armchairs. She had a naturally happy disposition and preferred to live in the present. Happiness immunized her from the past—for why look back for what has slipped from one's possession?—and from the future, which may never even be possessed. Perhaps never in the past, perhaps never in the future, had she been, could she be, so happy as she was now. The cuckoo woke her; she fell asleep to Lucy's purr. In the mornings he had usually left a dent beside her and gone out for his sunrising. Whatever one may say about bungalows, they are ideal for cats. She hunted his fleas on Sundays and Thursdays. He was now so strong and splendid that for the rest of the week he could perfectly well deal with them himself. She lived with carefree economy, seldom using more than a single plate, drinking water to save rinsing the teapot, and as far as possible eating raw foods, which entailed the minimum of washing up. Every Saturday she bought seven new-laid eggs, hard-boiled them, and spaced them out during the week—a trick she had learned from Vasari's *Lives of the Artists*. It was not an adequate diet for anyone leading an active life, but her life was calculatedly inactive—as though she were convalescing from some forgotten illness.

On Saturday evenings Mr. Bastable called to collect the rent and to see if anything needed doing—a nail knocked in or a tap tightened up. He always brought some sort of present: a couple of pigeons, the first tomatoes from his greenhouse, breakfast radishes. As the summer deepened, the presents enlarged into basketloads of green peas, bunches of roses, strawberries, sleek dessert gooseberries. But as the summer deepened and in spite of all the presents and economies, Aurelia's wealth of one hundred and twenty pounds lessened, and she knew she must turn her mind to doing something about this. She could not dig; there was no one but Mr. Bastable to beg from. The times were gone when one could take in plain sewing. Surveying the landscape she had come to take for granted, she saw the caravans in a new light—no longer peacefully grazing but fermenting with ambitions and cultural unrest.

By now they must have bought all the picture postcards at the shop. She had always wanted to paint. For all she knew, she might turn out to be quite good at it. Willows would be easy—think of all the artists who painted them. By now the caravaners must be tired of looking at real willows and would welcome a change to representational art. She took the bus to Wisbech, found an arts-and-crafts shop, bought paper, brushes, gouache paints, and a small easel. That same evening she did two pictures of willows—one tranquil, one storm-tossed. Three days later, she set up the easel on the outskirts of the caravan site and began a caravan from life. It was harder than willows—there were no precursors to inspire her—but when she had complied with a few suggestions from the caravan's owner she made her sale and received two further commissions. By the beginning of August she was rich enough to go on to oils—which was more fun and on the whole easier. It was remarkable how easily she painted, and with what assurance. The demand was chiefly for caravans. She varied them, as Monet varied his hay stacks. Caravan with buckets. Caravan with sunset. Pink caravan. One patron wanted a group of cows—though his children were cold toward them. She evaded portraits, but yielded to a request for an abstract. This was the only commission that really taxed her. Do as she might, it kept on coming out like a draper's window display. But she mastered it in the end, and signed it A. Lefanu like the rest.

By the end of September she had made enough to keep her in idleness till Christmas—when she would have thought of something else.

Winter would bring a new variety of happiness—slower, more conscious, and with more strategy in it. The gales of the equinox blowing across the flats struck at the spinney along the ridge, blew down one tree, and shook deadwood out of others. Here was an honest occupation. She set herself to build up a store of fuel against the winter. It was heavy work dragging the larger branches over the rough ground clogged with brambles and tall grass, but Lucy lightened it by flirting round her as she worked, darting after the tail of the branches, ambushing them and leaping on them as they rustled by. She was collecting fuel, Lucy was growing a thick new coat; both of them were preparing their defenses against the wintry months ahead. Mr. Bastable said that by all the signs it would be a hard winter, preceded by much rain and wind. He advised her to get her wood in before the rain fell and made the ground too soggy to shift it. If she manages the first winter, he thought, she will settle. Though she was an ungrateful tenant, or at any rate an inattentive receiver, he wanted her to settle; it delighted him to see her making these preparations. Later on, he would complete them by chopping the heavier pieces into nice little logs. Taking Mr. Bastable's advice, Aurelia decided to get the wood in, working on till the dusk was scythed by the headlights of passing cars, till Lucy vanished into a different existence of being a thing audible—a sudden plop or a scuffling. She never had to call him when she went indoors. By the time she was on the threshold he was there, rubbing against her, raising his feet in a ritual exaggeration. He was orderly in his ways, a timekeeper. He took himself in and out, but rarely strayed. When she came back from selling those unprincipled canvases, he was always waiting about for her, curled up on the lid of the water butt, drowsing under the elder, sitting primly on the sill of the window left open for him. He was happy enough out of her sight, but he liked to have her within his.

So she told herself, later on, that foggy, motionless November evening when he had not come in at his usual time. She had kindled a fire, not that it was cold—indeed, it was oddly warm and fusty; but the fog made it cheerless. It was a night to pull the curtains closer, listen to the snap and crackle of a brief fire, go early to bed. She had left the curtains unclosed, however. If Lucy saw that a fire had been kindled, he would be drawn from whatever busied him. He was a very chimney-corner cat, although he was a tom. Twice the brief fire died down, twice she made it up again. She went to the door, peered uselessly into the fog, called him. It was frightening to call into that silent, immediate obscurity.

"Lucy. Lucy."

She waited. No Lucy. She must resign herself to it. Tonight Lucy was engaged in being a tom. As she stood there, resigning herself to it and straining her ears, she felt the damp of the foggy air pricked with a fine drizzling rain. A minute later, the rain was falling steadily; not hard but steadily. She had not the courage to go on calling. The pitch of her voice had frightened her; it sounded so anxious. She went indoors and sat down to wait. On a different night she would have left

the window open and gone to bed, and in the morning Lucy
would have been there, too, and in her sleep her arm would
have gone out and round him.

With the rain, it had become colder. She added coal to the
fire. It blazed up but did not warm her. She counted the blue
pottery birds and listened. She listened for so long that finally
she became incapable of listening, and when there was a
sound which was not the interminable close patter of rain she
did not hear it, only knew that she had heard something. A
dragging sound . . . the sound of something being dragged
along the path to the door. It had ceased. It began again.
Ceased.

When she snatched the door open, she could see nothing
but the rain, a curtain of flashing arrows lit by her lighted
room. A noise directed her—a tremulous yowl. He struck at
her feebly when she stooped to pick him up, then dragged
himself on into the light of the doorway. She fell on her knees.
This sodden shapeless thing was Lucy. He looked at her with
one eye; the other sagged on his cheek. His jaw dangled. One
side of his head had been smashed in; his front leg was broken. When she touched him he shrank from her hand and
yowled beseechingly. Slowly, distortedly, he hitched himself
over the threshold, across the room, tried to sit up before the
fire, fell over, and lay twitching and gasping for breath. When
at last she dared touch him, his racing heartbeats were like a
machine fastened in him. She talked to him and stroked his
uninjured paw. He did not shrink from her now, and perhaps
her voice lulled him as the plumpness of his muscular soft
paw lulled her, for he relaxed and curled his tail round his
flank as though he were preparing to fall asleep. Long after he
seemed to be dead, the implacable machine beat on. Then it
faltered, stumbled, began again at a slower rate, fluttered. A
leaden tint suffused his eye and his lolling tongue. His breathing stopped. He flattened. It was inconceivable that he could
ever have been loved, handsome, alive.

"Lucy!"

The cry broke from her. It unloosed another.

"Aurelia!"

She could not call back the one or the other. She was Lucy Ridpath, looking at a dead cat who had never known her.

The agony of dislocation was prosaic. She endured it because it was there. It admitted no hope, so she endured it without the support of resentment.

The rain had gone on all the time and was still going on. Lucy Ridpath's mackintosh was hanging in the closet, ready to meet it. Mrs. Barker had advised her to put it on and she had done so. Tomorrow she would put it on again when she went out to dig a hole in the sodden ground for the cat's burial. It is proper to bury the dead; it is a mark of respect. Lucy would bury Lucy, and then there would be one Lucy left over.

She sat in the lighted room long after the light of day came into it. Then she put on the mackintosh and took up the body and carried it out. The air was full of a strange roar and tumult, a hollow booming that came from everywhere at once. The level landscape was gone. The hollow booming rose from a vast expanse and confusion of floodwater. Swirling, jostling, traversed with darker streaks, splintering into flashes of light where it contested with an obstacle, it drove toward the river. Small rivulets were flowing down from the ridge to join it, the track to the road was a running stream. In all that water there must be somewhere a place to drown.

With both hands holding the cat clasped to her bosom, she walked slowly down the track. When she came to the road, the water was halfway to her knees. A little farther along the road there was a footbridge over the roadside ditch. It was under water but the handrail showed. She waded across it. The water rose to her knees. With the next few steps she was in water up to her thighs. It leaned its ice-cold indifferent weight against her. When a twig was carried bobbing past her,

she felt a wild impulse to clutch it. But her arms were closed
about the cat's body, and she pressed it more closely to her
and staggered on. All sense of direction was gone; sometimes
she saw light, sometimes she saw darkness. The hollow booming hung in the air. Below it was an incessant hissing and
seething. The ground rose under her feet; the level of water
had fallen to her knees. Tricked and impatient, she waded
faster, took longer strides. The last stride plunged her forward.
She was out of her depth, face down in the channel of a stream.
She rose to the surface. The current bowed her, arched itself
above her, swept her onward, cracked her skull against the
concrete buttress of a revetment, whirled the cat out of her
grasp.

THE QUALITY OF MERCY

On an impulse, the boy got up, and saying to his friends, "Back presently," crossed the room and sat down at the table to which the young woman had just returned, walking unsteadily from the bar counter with her fourth whisky. He supposed the impulse to be sudden; in fact, it was the crest of a compulsion which had been gathering force in him during the last quarter of an hour. Now he curled his hand round the glass and pulled it toward him.

"Excuse me."

She started. Seeing her glass on his side of the table, she paled with rage. But mastering herself, she replied, "That's all right. Your necessity's greater than mine."

Her speech was thick but she spoke in an educated voice. She was, what he hadn't expected, a lady. Further, and this too he had not expected, she was considerably older than he. Studying her from a distance, he had taken her to be no more than a kid. The untidy tendrils of soft pale hair, the air of inconsequence, poverty, and recklessness, were youthful; and to be wearing a coat so much too large for her slender frame, a coat that might have been passed on to her by a rich aunt, that was youthful, too. But actually, she was quite an age—thirty or forty, he supposed.

Having committed himself, he could only go on.

"Johnnie! A tomato juice for the lady."

The barman brought it and pocketed the money without comment. The *El Dorado* was a place where anyone might get off with anyone. Every English provincial town has such an establishment, showy in a back street, decorated with some degree of sophistication, licensed for drinks and light refreshments, and frequented by the young because it is at once more refined and more raffish than the public houses their parents go to. He knew the boy, a young tough called Danny, and the group he came with. The woman he had never seen before and wouldn't be sorry if he never saw again. She was a misfit; and the *El Dorado* wasn't geared for misfits.

Impaled on the same reflection, the boy said, "Have I seen you here before?"

"No. I've been away. But this is my native town."

"Is it really?"

She did not answer.

"Born here, and all that?"

"Born and bred in a briar patch."

God alone knew what she meant. Her glance hovered on the whisky, and he tightened his hand round the glass.

"Why did you take away my whisky?"

"Reasons of my own."

"Hypothetical reasons."

Confusing hypothetical with highfalutin, he frowned. Answering the frown, she continued; "Obviously hypothetical since it's still there. The only practical reason would be that you wanted to drink it yourself."

And do I want to, he thought, evading its limpid hazel eye.

"So you've been going round the town celebrating your return?"

"Till you spoilt my little game."

Her laugh bared her teeth, she looked ready to bite him.

He could feel the grins at the table he had quitted burning
into his back. Her hand flashed out, quick as a viper. Just in
time, he withdrew the glass, and since there seemed no alternative, he drank off the whisky.

"Danny's in! Danny falls for the umpteenth time." He heard
his friends sniggering, and their grins burned deeper into his
back. This was what you let yourself in for, fancying you can
be a Good Samaritan. You go off the drink, for more than
three weeks you keep off it—and because of a soppy impulse
to salvage a poor kid who turns out to be nothing of the sort,
you're landed with having to drink her whisky.

Rage made him speak insultingly. "And where have you
been hiding yourself, all this long time?"

"I had a job in London—but it came to an end."

Easy to see why.

"A puppet theater—I played the guitar and kept the ac-
counts. But we couldn't keep going. And then . . ." She ram-
bled on as though talking to the wind, how this went wrong
and that became impossible. In spite of the fortuity of her nar-
rative it was always easy to see why.

"And the doctor, such a kind man, I found out he was a
Zen Buddhist, said I must have a quiet country life. So I came
down on Friday—my sister's taken me in. But I mean to get
back!"

The last words came out in a squawk, propelled by her
tears. In desperation, she gulped some tomato juice, comment-
ing, "Any port in a storm."

"That's right. Like a smoke?"

"Dying for one."

As he leaned forward to light the cigarette, he noticed how
the tears on her cheeks reflected minute tinsel images of the
flame.

"That's enough about me. Now tell me about yourself."

"Soon told. I'm nineteen, I've got a good clean home, I

work for a builder, and I booze. Actually, I haven't lost my
job yet. But I've been up three times for being drunk and disorderly, and next time it won't be so good."

"Oh. Was that why you came over to my table?"

"Sort of."

"Alcoholics Anonymous."

Now her voice was cold and her manner detached. She was
retreating behind the barrier of her class, and if he had chosen, he could have got away. But he did not choose.

He said, "Nothing to laugh at. They're good people.
They've got the right idea, anyhow."

"That we can help one another?"

"That no one else can."

She nodded; but immediately her face took on a repelling
expression, and she inquired, almost derisively and yet beguil-
ingly, "Were you very drunk? And *very* disorderly?"

"Blind drunk. Killing drunk."

She flinched.

"That's how I am, when I'm drunk. That's what it will
come to, one of these days."

Like the moon coming out of a cloud, he thought, like a
face on the screen fading out and another looking through it.
For she had dropped all her airs and disguises, and the real
woman (he had no doubt it was the real woman) had emerged
and declared herself and was looking at him with the childish
sternness of someone by nature very timid.

"You oughtn't to say that, even to me. It's not true. You
only say it to bolster yourself up, because you are young, and
so lonely. But it's not true. Not yet."

"Not yet."

"Exactly. Not yet. Well, that's a foothold, isn't it? Instead of
saying, 'It will come to killing, one of these days,' you should
say to yourself, every night, 'Thank God I haven't killed.' It
would be much more in harmony with your feelings, for
you're a kind person by nature. I could see that, when you

came to sit with me, and ordered the tomato juice. Not many people would have troubled to do that. What made you do it?"

"Well, I thought you'd had about enough, and that probably you weren't—"

He broke off, abashed. He had so nearly said, old enough.

"Go on."

". . . that you didn't—"

"Go on."

"Well, that you hadn't—that you hadn't been at it long enough to know much about it."

"That I was young enough to be worth helping, that I might still pull up? No. But you, you are young enough. Can't you try? You've been so kind to me, I really would like to be a warning to you. Do try!"

The barman was going to and fro, collecting glasses and emptying ash trays. Reaching their table, he picked up the emptied whisky glass, hesitated disdainfully over the half-finished tomato juice.

"Done with it?"

"I'm not preaching," she said, disregarding the inquiry. The humility in her voice released Danny from an agony of embarrassment during which he had been thinking, "Now she'll want us to try together."

"Well, actually, I don't mind telling you I have been trying. It's three weeks and two days since I touched a drop—barring putting away your rightful . . ."

"O my God!"

The exclamation was so rapid, so furtive, that if he had not seen her stricken countenance he might not have known he had heard it.

"Don't worry yourself about that. It won't make any difference."

"No difference!"

"I swear it shan't," he said vehemently.

It was closing time. All round them people were getting up, and shafts of cold air drove in as the door opened and shut. She made no move.

"Have you far to go?"

"Not really very far. Edgecombe Road, the farther end."

She rose, her coat straggling from her shoulders.

"I'll help you in. You'll want it, it's a cold night." He took hold of the coat, and at the same moment she vanished from within it, and was sitting down once more.

"I can't stand very well. Oh! There's my bag."

He turned to the group of his friends who were watching from the doorway.

"Here, Louis! Lend a hand. The rest of you can get out."

Together, he and Louis shoved her into her coat and hauled her through the doorway.

"She'll be better, once she feels the air," he said, knowing too well that this was a fallacy.

"Oh, will she? Where are we taking her to?"

"Far end of Edgecombe Road."

"Whew! Nice sight we'll make in that respectable neighborhood. I say, Danny! Won't do for us to meet the cops. We'll have to go roundabout."

They went by alleys and byways, twice making a detour to avoid a policeman on his beat, often crossing the road to forestall a face-to-face meeting with other belated walkers. Whenever they stopped to debate which way to turn next, she regained a hold on her consciousness, apologized for having such silly legs, and thanked them with a rambling graciousness for being so kind to her. This made them hurry on, for when they walked she fell silent, and seemed in a stupor—so that at intervals they conversed about her as though it were a straw dummy they dragged along between them, a badly made straw dummy bits of which were flapping and threatening to come loose.

"She must have put away a lot before ever she came to the

El, that's my opinion. Look out! We don't want no dogs after us."

"Tiger, Tiger! Come here at once!" The lady taking out her terrier saw with relief that they were disappearing down Meeting House Lane.

"You know, Danny, I'm beginning to think we'd better turn back and take her to the hospital. We can't knock at every door in Edgecombe Road and say, 'Excuse me, does this lady belong here?' "

"We haven't got there yet."

This truth was unexpectedly reinforced by a voice interpolating, "But my sister doesn't live anywhere near the gasworks."

"Where does she live?" inquired Louis, who was the quick-witted one.

"Edgecombe Road."

"Any particular number?"

"A hundred and thirteen. But on the gate it's Lilliesleaf. A place we used to go to when we were children. Nowhere near the gasworks."

"She's slipped off again," said Louis. "But she's coming round. She'll be more or less herself before we hit Lilyleaf. Pretty voice she's got, too. You wouldn't think it, really."

The pretty voice remarked, "I'm going to be sick."

When they had tidied her up and assured her that now she'd do fine, they set on once more, but had to go back to look for her bag which she dropped during her vomit, and which they had overlooked. It had been splashed, and while Danny was rubbing it on a grass verge, the town clock told midnight.

"Oh heavens! Was that twelve?"

"Don't worry. We won't turn into pumpkins. Here's your bag."

"I know what you will turn into. You'll turn into angels." Her spirits were rising, and she had got back some use of her legs, though she still could not walk straight. Once more they left the gasworks behind them. Ten minutes later they came to the railway bridge, where the wind whined in the cutting.

"One of our puppet turns was a porter, and the trunk was on a wire of its own, so whenever he tried to lift it—Wait a minute. I think the quickest way to Edgecombe Road is on the right."

"Hush! So's the cop. Sorry to take you out of your way, but it won't do for our Danny to cause remark. Turning cold, isn't it?"

Presently they were in the politer part of the town, where the houses stood separately and afforded less shelter from the wind. When they rounded the corner into the Edgecombe Road, they met the full force of it, and drew closer together.

"And your place is right at the top?"

"Yes. Look. I'm feeling so much better, let me go the rest of the way by myself."

"This isn't a road where I'm what you might call on my native heath in," said Louis. "So I'd like to see more of it. Same for Danny, I'm sure."

The houses at the lower end of the Edgecombe Road were Victorian, tall and massive, with spectral conservatories attached, and standing each in its large garden. It took a long time to go from one to the next. Some were for sale, with house-agents' boards rearing out of unpruned laurels; all were lightless, morose, implacably respectable. Ahead was a church with an ornamental spire and a plain-faced clock in it. By the time they drew level the hands stood at 12:16. Soon after the church, the Victorian houses were succeeded by a variety of Edwardian villas. These were smaller, and gave an illusion of ground gained; but the gardens were almost equally large so the illusion soon faded. Then came an open space, laid out in tennis courts and lawns. Then, after a dozen more villas, and a petrol station fronting a cemetery, the houses became contemporary, of meaner proportions and placed near to the road. All were lightless, spruce, and implacably respectable; but their respectability was alerter and more tight-lipped.

"Not far now," said Louis consolingly. He sensed that consolation was needed. There was no answer. Danny was thinking how much better it would have been to have fallen in with the suggestion of the hospital. The woman's faculties were concentrated in her gaze that searched ahead to where a chink of light had momentarily appeared in a ground-floor window. Where the chink had been there loomed a faint curtained glow. Margaret was sitting up.

"This is it."

Danny unlatched the gate.

"I shall never be able to tell you how grateful—"

A bright light was switched on in the hall, the door was flung open.

"Fanny! Where on earth have you been? Do you know what time it is?"

"O Margaret, I'm so sorry. We came as fast—"

"We?"

Margaret stood on the top step, blinking angrily into the darkness. The light delineated her small trim figure and shone down on her rigidly waved yellow hair.

"We?"

Danny came forward.

"We brought the lady back. She wasn't feeling too good."

"O Margaret, they've been so kind to me, especially this one. He's Danny, the other's Louis. They've come all this way, and it's so horribly cold, and I'm sure you've got a kettle on, you'd never be without a kettle—"

"What's that on your skirt?"

"—so can my guardian angels have some tea?"

"You're drunk. You filthy, stinking, drunken beast, you stand there gabbling about guardian angels, when you ought to be ashamed to show your face. All these hours I've been waiting for you! Little you care! I took you in when nobody else would; I washed your filthy clothes; I listened to your excuses and your repentances. And the first moment I take my eye off you, you rush out for another wallow, and disgrace yourself in front of half the town. Oh, you're worthless, worthless, worthless! The gutter's too good for you."

She raged, and her hair remained in its rigid undulations, placid as a wig. "And then, as if that wasn't enough, you trail home with these two sots, and have the effrontery—"

"No! How dare you speak like that? It's not right, it's not just. They're good, they're kind, they've done everything they can to help me. Danny even drank my whisky."

"That I can well believe."

"But, Margaret— Oh, it's hopeless, you'll never understand. Oh, I wish I were dead!"

"I wish I had a pair of tongs."

She was dragged up the steps. On the top step she tripped, and fell on her knees. Still on her knees, she shuffled round and said into the darkness, "I'm sorry my sister doesn't know how to behave."

"In with you! And as for you two, I'm going to report you to the police."

The door was slammed. They heard the noise of furious altercation behind it, and then, from the curtained room, the clicking of a telephone dial.

BRUNO

"And do I go down this?"

Bruno paused before the pair of stone gateposts, one topped with a wolf, the other with half a wolf. The gate had been pinned open with a notice-board saying PRIVATE.

"Keep to the right after the bend," said Gilbert.

The narrow rutted drive went steeply downhill. The rhododendrons bulging on either side made it narrower still. Their wet foliage swished against the car. Behind their exterior abundance they were cavernous with neglect. Hens were scratching about beneath them. At the bend a couple of hens decided to cross the drive.

"—Henryson's, I suppose. He's my factor. That's his house down there."

The ruts continued towards Henryson's house. The main drive crossed a small deep-set stream, traversed a plantation of conifers, came to a second gate. This too had been propped open. Beyond it was a space of gravel where it was possible to draw up with something like a flourish. The two men sat in the car, Gilbert Brodie contemplating the home of his forebears, Bruno the house which he had been given to understand might ultimately become his. Squat, darkling, battlemented, it was not even ludicrous. It was too remote to be turned into a hotel, and too small to sell to a religious com-

munity. Discarding all interest in it, he exclaimed, "It's pure
Lucia di Lammermoor! Gibbie, I shall have to call you Edgardo."

The car creaked and tilted as Gibbie eased himself out, his
stick menacing Bruno's shins. Even making allowance for the
bulk of opera singers, Edgardo was a misnomer.

The front door—massy oak with iron studs—was opened by
a very thin woman with a high forehead and faded red hair,
whom Gilbert greeted as Mrs. Henryson. "And here is my
friend, Mr. Bonsella. It's his first visit to Scotland."

"Henryson was sorry he couldn't be here just now, Mr. Gilbert. He's away to the electricity. You're in the east room, like
you said, and Mr. Bouncer next door." With surprising
strength she picked up the two valises and carried them up
the pitch-pine staircase. Bruno made a belated dart after her,
then desisted. She heard their voices going away into the
study, and the young man saying, "What a spread! I've always
heard about Scotch teas, and now . . ." She stood on the
landing, shaking her head. It was over ten years since she had
seen Gilbert, and he was not the better for them.

In the study Gilbert was repeating what he had already told
Bruno a great many times.

"—After her funeral I stayed on, burning her old hats,
water-colors, stuffed animals. Then I had it properly reno-
vated, electricity everywhere, all the new labor-saving gadgets,
two bathrooms, new fences, lots of roses—my mother only
grew roses on her hats—new gates. It hadn't been in the
agent's hands for a week before he had a tenant for it. All
smiles to begin with. Then the usual story. After the third lot
I washed my hands of it. Then, this New Year—just before I
found you, Bruno—I began to think what a fool I was, living
in one exorbitant hotel after another, always looking out of
different windows at the same boring Mediterranean, while I
had a perfectly good house eating its head off, and Henryson
coining money with my grouse and my partridges while I was

paying twenty francs for half a frozen rook. And so— Do you take sugar? I ought to know by this time, oughtn't I, but I've got no head nowadays."

He lifted the heavy silver teapot with a shaking hand, and spilled the tea over the cloth. "This damned teapot has never poured straight."

"Marvelous jam! I suppose it's homemade," said Bruno, helping himself to more of it. "I haven't eaten such jam since I was an innocent child." His host sat pouting at the stain on the tablecloth. He was in his own house, there was no one to rebuke him; but as the stain spread outwards, he felt rebuked.

Gilbert Brodie was experienced in rebukes. He was the son who wasn't killed in the war. No fault of his. He had joined the Royal Air Force in 1918—the quickest way to an estimable death; but there just wasn't time for it. When he came on leave after the Armistice his widowed mother flung her arms round him, exclaiming, "You are all I've got left."

This was in the hall, overlooked by the glassy stare of dead stags, foxes, otters, badgers, two large pike, and a wildcat (the birds were in the gun room). These, and the place and his mother were his inheritance. Extricating an arm from her embrace, he patted her sturdy back. The embrace fell off. He had done the wrong thing.

And so it continued. His good intentions went awry, his good ideas were inapplicable, his consolations were inappropriate, his jokes fell flat. His wants were too simple to be allowed.

What he wanted was to live at home, quarrel with nobody, kill nothing, and write a novel about school life. As a step toward this he disgraced himself out of the Air Force by threatening to load his plane with butter and fly it to Germany. When he came home after this his mother ordered him out of her house. It was in fact his house but he was feeling too unwell to chop logic with her. He went off to the village inn and had measles. Measles, at a time when everybody had been

dying so dramatically of Spanish Influenza, was the wrong
thing again. But the inn people were kind to him and for
some months he was perfectly happy, helping behind the bar,
looking after the pony, and writing his novel. Then his
mother, who judged that by now Gilbert would have learned
his lesson, forgave him and told him to return. It was summer.
He thought of the large rooms, the linen sheets, and agreed.
The servants, whose hearts he had not broken, welcomed him
back. His mother was out a good deal of the time, organizing
things for disabled ex-servicemen. Though not perfectly
happy, he was happy enough. It was not till the second winter
after this that he began to drink.

He did not drink more than a Scottish landowner or a retired warrior might do unblamed, and it made his relations
with his mother considerably easier. In the spring he bought a
car. It was called a Trojan, and had solid tires.

It was after this assertion of manliness that Mrs. Brodie decided it was her duty to become a grandmother. Gilbert's second cousin was invited to stay, and after inspection was invited to stay longer. The girl was modern, of course; but when
time had stripped her of her long earrings and her long
cigarette holder, she would do. Meanwhile, her modernity
would give Gilbert a shake-up, which was what he needed.
Mrs. Brodie exerted herself to please. She showed off family
possessions, told family scandals as though to a mature
woman, pinned a paste brooch on the promising bosom, and
had the piano tuned. Insensibly, she and her nominee got into
a way of laughing at Gilbert and making a party against him.
"You'll hurt poor Gilbert's feelings." "Impossible! He's got
solid tires!"

Gilbert laughed too. But an hour later, while the girl was
passing away a wet afternoon with her repertory of songs from
The Beggar's Opera, he packed his best clothes and the manu-
script of his novel, which only needed finishing, and loaded
the Trojan. As he got in his mother threw open a window and

said, "Where are you off to, Gilbert? I've got a parcel I want left at Mrs. Todd's and while you are about it you can take back that tinned pinapple to Oliphant's and tell him I ordered slices, not chunks." "I'm going to London," he said, and drove away.

This had long been a cherished proud memory. He could not picture Bruno behaving with such spirit. Bruno had no initiative, no spirit of adventure. His car stood neglected in the garage for days on end, for he was daunted by the British rule of the road and the many miles between petrol stations. He flinched at a drop of rain and mistrusted any animal larger than a sheep. But in one's sixties one has given up, if not hoping for perfection, at least expecting it. Bruno was a hearthrug cat: a handsome, bright-eyed, lissome specimen whose air of well-being would make him a credit to any owner. The friends of one's youth, to whom one pledges an unthinking heart, desert one—or somehow one has deserted them. The adoptions of one's middle age, the prancing harlequins, the engaging little gold diggers, the splendid, sentimental, self-righteous, mother-loving, dunderheaded objects of a Walt-Whitmanesque devotion, wring one's vitals, one's purse, one's patience, and are gone. One says, "Good riddance," and in secret licks one's wounds; and in a profounder secrecy contemplates the reach-me-down expedients of old age. All things considered, especially the two ghastly misadventures which had preceded Bruno, Gilbert could think himself lucky to be back on his own hearth with such an amiable companion: amiable, and with every promise of being reliable. Bruno, a hearthrug cat, would not be lissome forever, but he would be constant, since he had not the enterprise to be anything else. If either of us breaks it off, thought Gilbert, it won't be Bruno. At this, his spirits gave a queer little skip of satisfaction.

Tea, and the stained cloth, had been cleared away, when Henryson came in. His tale was pretty much what Gilbert expected: the wettest spring for five years, grouse disease, the barley running all to straw, poachers, broken fences, leaking roofs, gates off their hinges, the woodwork perishing for lack of paint. Bruno on the window seat with his feet up added, "The roses need pruning." Henryson shot him a yellow glance. Seeing this, Gilbert found his spirits giving another little skip.

After a few days, Bruno, thinking it over (he had never in his life had so much time for thought) decided that Henryson was a blessing in disguise. Gibbie would tire of being at the beck and call of this malodorous man, tire of being dragged out to stand for hours being lectured to and having his own view shouted down, tire of the creaking litany of Henryson's virtues and farsightedness and unappreciated labors, tire of being told that everything was wrong, tire of writing checks. He would give up this nonsense of being a landowner, turn his back on those battlements and drive away—as he had done on that famous first occasion, but now with Bruno doing the driving. They would go back to the Hotel Eblis. And Gibbie would be merry again, easily pleased, ridiculous, giggling like a schoolboy; a bore, of course; but a loving and rather touching bore. And not, above all, the only bore on the beach. It was the nonvariety of bores which made Bruno's present life so wearing. Even a wife would rebel. And he was not a wife.

At times, he could almost wish he were. If he had been a wife, he could have quarreled, and done so with a quiet mind, since nothing worse than alimony would have come of it. Or he could have cooked. He was fond of cooking, brooding over a béchamel, putting in the flavors. But his offers were rejected. Mrs. Henryson came in specially to cook for them. It would not do to hurt her feelings.

Another wifely escape was gardening. Gilbert's roses, a sullen scratchy lot, occupied a circular bed in the center of the lawn, ringed with wire netting. When he had weeded round them there was no more gardening he could undertake, since the lawn was mowed once a week by a boy with a harelip,

who also raked the gravel. The lawn had had its second mow-
ing before Bruno discovered the kitchen garden. It lay a quarter of a mile from the house within a high brick wall. Its gate
was kept locked; as a further precaution it was topped with
iron spikes. Peering between the bars, he saw lettuces, peas,
young carrots in disciplined rows, a tomato-house, a fruit-cage,
and at intervals dead birds swinging from gibbets. In the first
week Bruno would not have hesitated to demand the run of
his teeth among the tomatoes and peas and gooseberries—
small quantities of which were vouchsafed by Henryson and
implacably boiled by Mrs. Henryson. But now he had a
changed Gibbie, a northern Gibbie, to handle, so he resorted
to tablets of vitamin C, eked out by chewing sorrel and young
conifer tips. Bruno had been brought up to be healthy as
sternly as Victorian children were brought up to be good, and
when he drank too much or ate unadvisedly he was careful to
atone for it by an aperient. If poor Gibbie had followed the
same course, he would not be the gas-vat he now was.

Prescribing, too, could have been an occupation. When they
first took up together he had really done a lot for Gibbie, who
was in a shocking state. Lambswool for his hammertoes, slip-
pery elm for his stomach pains, valerian for his hangovers—
Bruno, whose health was flawless, was a great believer in nurs-
ery physic. Gibbie became a believer too, but lost his faith
after syrup of figs. On the other hand, a course of beauty cul-
ture did wonders. Layers of grime were eased out of his wrin-
kles, his scalp was frictioned, his eyebrows tailored. A slim-
ming course gave him a new interest in life which lasted for
over a fortnight. Then he went on the booze again, bungled
his hoist onto a barroom stool, slipped, hit his nose on the rail
—and was back where they'd started. Only the tailored eyebrows remained, and were embarrassing.

But there was no call for prescribing now. Gibbie throve in
his rude native air, stumped about in wet boots, ate like a
hog, snored all night, belched with enthusiasm, and sang in

his bath. It would not last. With Gibbie nothing lasted. It just happened that it was going on longer than one would have expected. Meanwhile, Bruno was reduced to reading books— at least to opening them to see if they were readable. In one of them he came on a person called Stockmar, who said he seemed to have come into the world in order to be of use to others. "Me to the life" Bruno commented, turned down the page and put the book back on the shelf.

Another thing which was going on longer than expected was Henryson's power to charm. He came in every morning, ostensibly to ask for orders, in fact to give them. Gibbie would go off with him, be out for hours, come back, puffing and blowing, to sit down at his desk, turn over catalogues with illustrations of drainpipes, write more checks. He complained as he wrote them, but with an abstract complaining. What with a labor government, nationalized railways which didn't deliver, overpaid workers striking for more pay, the country run by nincompoops and swindlers, etc., etc. . . . One afternoon when he had complained more than usual, Bruno thought the iron was sufficiently heated for a little tap to be administered.

"I suppose you are fattening him up to send him to the Agricultural Show."

"Fattening what up?"

"Henryson. Every day he gets something more out of you. Or is he just taking you for nature walks?"

Gilbert turned crimson, said nothing, remained crimson. For the rest of the day he sulked. The next morning he inquired with elaborate courtesy, "Would you have any objection, Bruno, if I went out with my factor to mark some trees for felling? After all, you'll be the gainer—ultimately."

"But, Gibbie—"

"Do you suppose it's for myself I am putting the place in order?"

To prove to himself that Bruno's words had no weight with him he told Henryson that on thinking it over he had decided

that it would be best to reroof the whole of Henryson's barn.
Even when Henryson replied, "Aye. I thought you would," he
did not waver. But when it came to marking the trees, his
heart was not in it. All the pleasures of ownership, of knowing
that the ground under his feet was his own ground, of smelling the remembered scent of the rushes by the loop of the
burn, of feeling the wind blowing out of the same wet quarter
and the turnips drenching his ankles and hearing Henryson's
captious whine like the voice of the landscape, were invali-
dated by Bruno's implication that he wasn't much of a master
after all. He should have come back sooner; or come back
without Bruno, who would sell the place as soon as he laid
hands on it. ". . . you'll be the gainer—ultimately." He
wished he had not said that: it was the sort of thing his
mother said. In fact, Bruno was not yet in his will. He had al-
tered it so often that he was shy of altering it again until he
had chosen a new lawyer.

Walking back from the plantation Henryson remarked,
"You'll be getting my niece this evening, Mr. Brodie."

"Your niece, Henryson?"

"She's my sister's girl. Mrs. Henryson finds the work getting
a bit beyond her, so while Deirdre's staying with us she'll be
coming for the evenings. She's from Glasgow."

Even apart from a Henryson niece being called Deirdre, this
was a disconcerting development. It was no business of Bruno's how many Henrysons might be about the place, but if he
chose to be tiresome, here was another incentive. Once and for
all, he must have it out with Bruno—if only because he didn't
want to quarrel with him.

"How old is your niece?"

"She's twenty-three."

Bruno was nineteen.

It was on his lips to say, "I won't have her."

In a confusion of resentments and apprehensions where the
only certainty was an imperative necessity to have it out with

Bruno, he entered the house—to be told by Mrs. Henryson that Mr. Bouncer had gone out in the car and would not be back to luncheon. He was then introduced to the niece. In the course of that long afternoon, Gilbert went through the usual vicissitudes of those who wait for a loved one. He thought Bruno was delaying in order to flout him, and was enraged. He thought Bruno had met with an accident, and was eaten by remorse. He knew he could do nothing, and counted the stony minutes. He was in the toilet when he heard a car draw up, its door slammed, the doorbell rung. There had been an accident. He had known it all along. Forcing himself to walk slowly he crossed the hall, opened the door. They had sent a woman to break the news. Calamities enact themselves like things long-before rehearsed, so it was no surprise to him that her face was vaguely familiar.

"Hullo, Gilbert. Do you remember me? I'm Lilah. May I come in?" she added when he did not move.

"Yes, yes, of course. Do come in. Nice to see you."

"I heard a rumor that you were back. And as I was in the neighborhood, opening a flower show, I thought I'd look in on the chance. Have you been back long?"

"Since June the tenth." (Bruno saying, "I shall have to call you Edgardo." Bruno, leaning out of the bedroom window, saying, how peaceful it was—and immediately sneezing.)

She had sat down and was looking round the room.

"What changes, Gilbert! I see you have got rid of quite a lot of ancestors. And the Bay of Naples."

"There are too many ancestors in Scotland."

"Your mother didn't think so. Poor Cousin Helen, how she used to put me through them, which were hers and which were Brodies. I'm glad you've kept the old dame in a turban. Which was she?"

"Isabella Brodie." (It was Bruno who found the portraits in the attic and insisted on hanging Isabella over the fireplace because she had a look of Gilbert.)

"Do you mind if I smoke?"

"I'm so sorry." He offered the cigarette box. She looked at his shaking hand and looked away.

"How it all comes back! It was out of this very window we saw you drive off to London. Gilbert, I won't say I blame you —but it was an awful thing to do."

"My mother's feelings?"

He could hear a car coming down the drive.

"Mine! Here I was, stuck, not able to get away, not knowing what to do, praying that the earth would open and swallow me up, looking at the Bay of Naples and knowing it wouldn't."

The car had drawn up. Bruno got out of it, carrying a great many paper bags.

"How did she take it? Was she awful? Do tell me!"

Bruno came in. Hearing Gibbie so cheerful and animated he felt considerable relief. He was introduced as "My secretary" to Miss Lilah Mackenzie, who said, "Mrs. Lumsden, if you please, Gilbert. I am a mother and a grandmother, so I have got out of the way of being Lilah Mackenzie."

Bruno did his secretary's bow, and proceeded to his secretary's task of offering drinks. Mrs. Lumsden was talking about her grandchildren. "But Hector's the flower of the flock."

"And how old is he?"

"Eleven. Red hair, green eyes, black lashes. No scholar, thank God, but he can do anything with his feet."

"You must bring him to see me."

"I mean to. I wouldn't let his rich bachelor relation slip through my fingers, believe you me."

"Well-bred," thought Bruno. "Only the well-bred are as coarse as that."

She went on to question Gibbie about the legacy which had made a rich relation of him. "How did you manage it, Gilbert? Cousin Helen said he couldn't endure you."

"He couldn't. But I was the only blood-Brodie left."

At this, for some unknown reason, they held up their wagging old heads and looked as proud as the castle Bruno had seen that afternoon.

A date was fixed for her visit. She drank a stiffish stirrup cup and drove away. Bruno produced his offerings: a pot of French mustard, a new kind of midge repellent, bull's-eyes and cinnamon balls from a wonderful period post office, a paperweight containing white heather, a handwoven tie, a pot of Gentleman's Relish, and a cactus. It was only after these had been admired and Bruno had taken the mustard and the Gentleman's Relish to the larder that Gilbert remembered Henryson's niece. He stiffened, and told himself he was under no obligation to account to Bruno for adding another Henryson to his retinue. Bruno returned, saying blandly, "Who's your jailbird?" Gilbert explained, thankfully taking the line that she was no choice of his. Bruno didn't want to quarrel either, and they spent the evening peacefully dicing for cinnamon balls.

Mrs. Lumsden and the grandchild were due in ten days' time. Bruno had hoped to spend the interval steering Gibbie toward the Hotel Eblis; but one languorous glance from Henryson's niece showed him he would have his work cut out if he was to keep Gibbie on an even keel. Her glutinous attention to his every word, the solicitude with which she put down his soup plate or gave an extra polish to his fork, her handmaid-of-the-Lord voice when she spoke of putting a hot-water bottle in his bed would have nauseated him at other times; now they made him tremble. There had already been occasions when Gibbie had a jealous fit. Bruno's nerves could not stand another. The situation was the more complicated since Gibbie was just as likely to be jealous of him as about him. He seemed to be impartially preparing to be either, and liable to blow up at any moment, when in a flash of vision Henryson's niece was presented to Bruno as a heaven-sent means to an end. Gilbert presently noticed that every evening (a time of day when Gilbert was wont to be forthcoming) Bruno became oddly silent and reserved; he developed a loud spasmodic cough and a quite new susceptibility to drafts; was continually getting up and going to the door to make sure it was properly closed. Inquiries about his health—it would be particularly awkward if he took sick just before Lilah and the boy came— were put by.

"Well, if you don't feel ill, what is it? Something's biting you."

Bruno looked at him, seemed about to speak, didn't.

"What's gone wrong? Have you got religion?"

Bruno began to listen intently, half rose.

"None of that door business, for God's sake! What is it, what have you got on your silly half-baked mind?"

"I'll tell you tomorrow. We'll go out for a drive, and then I'll tell you."

That night, saying to himself, "I'll do it yet," Bruno fell asleep like a child. Gilbert lay awake till dawn, swallowing sleeping pills and digestive tablets and scratching an outbreak of nettle rash.

Bruno waited till they had left the wolf and the half-wolf behind them.

"Gibbie, it's about Henryson's niece." His eyes were fixed on the road ahead but he heard Gilbert's breathing stagger. "I've been trying not to say anything about it. I've gone on hoping I was wrong. But I must. Gibbie, that girl has been planted on you. Ever since she came into the house, she's been bugging us."

Gilbert laughed. "I should have said it was you she had her eye on."

Bruno allowed a pause, long enough to be dignified.

"Your trouble, Gibbie dear, is that you have too much money to see what a wicked world you live in. You lead a sheltered life with everyone rooking you right and left. Even if you could hear that girl snorting through the keyhole whenever we're alone—you're the teeniest bit deaf, so you don't—

and scurrying away each time I get up to open the door, you'd say she'd been polishing the door handle. Take a fresh look at the Henrysons, Gibbie. They were doing quite tidily before you came back, selling your stuff, salting the money away, practically owning the place. What's happened since? New gates, new fences, new roofs—everything the heart of Henryson could wish. So you've put the place in order for them, and now all they've got to do is to get rid of you. So they send in their clever little niece to spy on our disgraceful doings— because nobody really likes being prosecuted for sodomy. . . . So I must go away, Gibbie."

He'd pitched his voice so exactly right that its composed sadness almost persuaded him he meant it; besides, he was un- used to uttering noble sentiments and found it gratifying. He patted Gilbert's knee, and continued, "I hate to hurt you— but there it is."

There was no sound from Gilbert.

"You've been so sweet to me, Gibbie, so generous—but it won't do, not here."

Still no sound from Gilbert.

"So I thought I'd go the day after tomorrow."

Gilbert said, "You're out of date. If you ever troubled to read a paper or listen to the news you'd know that all that is over and done with—small thanks to layabouts like you."

The Wolfenden Report and the inertia of the young occu- pied the rest of the drive. After putting the car in the garage, Bruno sat with his head in his hands, thinking about lunch- eons at the Eblis Hotel and cursing the Wolfenden Committee as a gang of interfering old busybodies. Gibbie was arch and cock-a-hoop all that day and Henryson's niece sang at the sink.

Two mornings later Gibbie remarked at breakfast, "Let's see. I think it's today you're leaving me for my good."

After this small spurt of malice, he turned his mind to all the things which must be done before the Lumsdens arrived. Most of this devolved on Bruno. When Gibbie had thought of bath salts for Mrs. Lumsden and ice cream for the boy his hospitality ran out.

They arrived. Bruno prepared himself for the sterner side of being a secretary. This included plucking and cleaning grouse in a whirl of feathers and bluebottles, since Henryson's niece would rather face a bull than a maggot. The boy was more stouthearted, and found maggots interesting and even a matter for congratulation. He would have taken on the grouse and asked no reward beyond entry to the kitchen and having something to do; but Bruno had a scruple of honor. He made an assault on Gilbert's vassalage to Henryson and demanded the key of the kitchen garden. As he made the assault publicly, he got it. He had not suspected figs; the bushes were not visible from the gate. While Hector rioted in the fruit-cage, he gorged on figs. No word was spoken between them and they walked silently back to the house. It was only on the threshold that the boy inquired, "Where did Cousin Gilbert find you?"

"He picked me up on a beach."

"Like a shell?"

"Like a beautiful shell," amended Bruno. The figs had restored his knowledge that he was beautiful. "And sometimes he puts his ear against my ribs and listens to the noise of the sea."

It was the first time he had heard the boy laugh unfeignedly; at intervals during lunch he caught Bruno's eye and giggles broke from him. Mrs. Lumsden glanced anxiously at Gilbert. Fortunately, Gilbert supposed that the giggles were provoked by his evocation of the day he drove off on his solid tires—he evoked it often—and made great play about the consternation he had left behind. "You'd never behave like that, would you, Hector?"

"Don't be so sure," said Hector's grandmother. "Hector's got a will of his own. He's quite a young spark already."

Bruno in his childhood had also been freely advertised. He had not minded it. But he saw that Hector was embarrassed

by his touting grandmother and did not like having to be
grateful so often to his Cousin Gilbert. She touted, Gilbert
acceded. Neither of them gave a thought to the child, who was
left to scratch up entertainment for himself, like the hens
under the rhododendrons. Not till the visit to the kitchen garden did it occur to Hector that Bruno, referred to by Mrs.
Lumsden as "that secretary person" and socially puzzling, since
he lived as an equal and was treated as an inferior, was an ac-
cessible companion. He fastened on him with a child's imperative wooing. Bruno would have preferred figs and time in his
own company, but companionship was forced upon him. They
bathed together and sailed paper boats down the burn—
Hector taught him how to make them; they climbed trees, explored about in the car, built a grotto, sat in the dank seclusion of the game larder telling ghost stories to an accom-
paniment of the steadfast buzzing of bluebottles worshiping
without; they carved their initials on trees, went out at dawn
to pick mushrooms, fled from hornets, swore eternal secrecies,
competed, leaning toward each other till they became almost of an age. And when the weather broke they sat in
the gun room composing an interminable strip cartoon where
each author in turn got Oxo and Rinso, its leading characters, into some irreparable situation and challenged the
other to get them out of it. Oxo and Rinso, rescued by a devoted polar bear from a band of Russian explorers who had
designs on the magnetic pole, had escaped on an iceberg,
which melting on the shores of Italy had left them to be im-
prisoned in a cruel orphanage which Bruno had to get them
out of. Bruno was managing this by means of an earthquake
and a traveling ballet company. Rinso, hanging head down
from a tottering arch, was keeping the bear erect by dangling
a bun while Oxo ran round it with a tutu. Hector was min-
gling heavy breathings with squeals of delight; the bear, enter-
ing into the spirit of the thing, had just performed its first *en-
trechat;* the door was flung open and there stood Gibbie, who

said, "Come out, Bruno! I've got something to say to you."
The hair on his upper lip bristled. His eyes were dwindled
in his head. His face was blotched with irrational patches of
scarlet. It quivered and was contorted, but for some time his
rage would not let him speak. At last he got at the word
"scum."

"You scum, you scum, you scum, you scum! You filthy, re-
volting pervert, you body louse! Do you think I haven't seen
what you are up to with the boy? You'd corrupt him, would
you? I might have known it. *My* boy, I tell you! My decent,
clean-minded, innocent boy. My heir, who I've found at last.
Who I can give the rest of my life to. Who won't betray me,
or sneer at me, or keep in with me for what he can get out of
it. Do you suppose I didn't know what you were up to, sneak-
ing off into the woods, bathing naked, cutting your initials on
my trees, showing him those disgusting drawings, tickling
his . . ."

"*Pas devant les enfants,*" said Bruno mildly.

All this time he had kept firm hold of the door handle,
which was being wrenched at from the other side. Now he
let go. Hector rushed out, reiterating "You beast, you beast,
you beast!" and pinched Gibbie in the stomach. Mrs. Lumsden appeared. Bruno ran upstairs saying he must wash his
hands before lunch.

Washed and manicured, he joined the party and made al-
laying remarks when they were called for. Gibbie, looking
very unwell, spoke kindly to the boy. Mrs. Lumsden broke in
before the boy could answer, talking loudly and gaily and pro-
moting an impression that he was too young to speak for himself. She'll skin him as soon as she can get him alone, thought
Bruno; then she'll lock him up on bread and water. After all,
it was she he hated most. While she was skinning her grand-
son, Gibbie, if he had any sense, would put his feet up. It
would not be a difficult departure. No one was likely to throw
himself in front of the car, and he had very little to pack. He

must remember to get the tank filled up at Gibbie's petrol station and charged to Gibbie. He packed, scouted from the stairhead, went down, through the hall and out of the door unobserved. Squat, darkling, battlemented, the home of Gibbie's forebears was behind him. Gibbie's example, that moldy, clanking legend, was before him. Like Gibbie, he was about to drive away. For good. The wolf and the half-wolf, the family portraits, the pitch-pine Gothic, the hens and the rhododendrons and belching, scratching, stinking old Gibbie would never see him again. He was through with the lot of them. It was the holiday season; he had the car and his clothes—he always took care of his clothes; he could get along in four languages; something would turn up.

It was raining as hard as ever. By the time he got to the garage his hair was plastered to his forehead. He put his valise into the hold, got in, started the engine. Two wet red hands pawed on the window. "Hold on, Bruno! I'm coming too. Where shall we go?"

"You'll see."

It was the boy who sounded the horn as the car swept past the house.

Ten minutes later, Mrs. Lumsden put out her cigarette and went to release Hector. Never again must he be so rude to Gilbert; on the other hand it would not do to set the child against his cousin, or he would be ruder than ever. She unlocked the door. A wet curtain flapped in the open window. He had scrambled down by the ivy, then jumped; she could see his neat arriving footmarks. She put on her raincoat and went in search. Not in the house. Not in the visible garden. He might be anywhere in the grounds. "Hector! Hector!" He might stay out all night to flout her—he was capable of it. And in this rain. She called louder, thinking what her daughter-in-law would say if Hector got pneumonia and the legacy miscarried—which it might well do if Gilbert were put to the trouble of a sick child in the house. Mrs. Henryson came from the back door in a mackintosh. "Are you crying on Master Hector, ma'am? He's away. He went off in the car with Mr. Bouncer. I heard the horn and looked out and saw them. Master Hector was holding the wheel and I can't say I think it's very safe."

Gilbert's bedroom window was thrown up. "What's all this yelling and chattering, Lilah? How can I get a wink of sleep? And why are you standing there, getting soaked?"

"Mrs. Henryson was telling me that Hector had gone off in the car with your Mr. Bonsella—and that he was being allowed to steer it. I must say I think that young man takes too much on himself. It isn't as if the car were an ordinary runabout. You must have paid a fortune for it."

An extraordinary sort of groan came from Gilbert, and he disappeared from the window. She went in to the house and saw him lurching down the stairs with the speed of a crab.

"He's gone off with him, the sod! Blast him, blast him! Why wasn't I told? I'm never told anything. Why the hell could you not keep an eye on him, Lilah? Have I got to do everything? You brought him here, the least you could do was to look after him. We must go after them at once—God knows which way they'll have gone. Get your car from the garage, quick!"

"Why don't you ring up the police?"

"What good would that do? The police are hopeless. Anyhow, I don't know the number of the car."

"Not know the number of your own car? Really, Gilbert, you are a prize lily of the field."

"It's *his* car."

"*His car?* That car his car? How on earth can he afford a car like that?"

"I gave it to him."

When she brought her Austin round she heard him telephoning. The receiver was slammed down, Gilbert came out.

"No answer."

"No answer from the police?"

"I was trying to get Henryson."

"Get in," she said. And seeing him in difficulties she took hold of his collar and hauled him in like a sheep. "It's my belief all this is a fool's errand," she said bitterly.

The car jolted along the drive, over the bridge, up the slope.

"Which way—" She swerved, braked violently, came to a stop among smashing rhododendrons. A few yards ahead lay Hector, face down.

"Hector! What's the matter? Are you hurt?"

"This is as far as you're coming," Bruno had said. "Get out."

"But why? What's the idea?"

"You'll see."

"You said that before. Bruno, you swine!"

He was pushed out. Smiling like an Indian god, Bruno said, "Have a good time," and drove on.

He ran after the car. It was as though he were blowing it away from him like a soap bubble. When it was out of sight, he still ran. When he could run no more, he stood looking along the road. An approaching van hooted at him to get out of its way and as it passed the driver exclaimed, "Idiot!" He turned and walked back to the gateposts and entered the drive. There his dignity left him. Raging and humiliated, he threw himself down, and screamed and kicked and tore up the wet grass. Long after, he heard them saying, "Hector! What's the matter? Are you hurt?" and scorned to answer.

A VISIONARY GLEAM

In Memory of MILLICHAMP HOWEL
Artist and Benefactor
Born at Llanyspytty Hen 1st May 1866
Died at Davos 7th Jan. 1933
Si Monumentum Requiris Circumspice

Jeremy had already been looking round the church of Llanyspytty for some time. He had looked at the east window and
the west window, the pulpit and the font cover. He had examined the organ case. He had studied the reredos. It was obvious that all these sprang from one mind, one feverish half-
baked mind. His eyes, dizzied by peacock-blue crags,
tinned-salmon-colored flesh tints, writhing scrolls, arum lilies,
and mauve beards, had turned to the mural tablet merely for
relief, asking nothing of it except that it should remain white
marble and calm. But subconsciously he must have absorbed
the inscription, for when its import steadied into a meaning it
was as though he had known Millichamp Howel for quite a
long time.

Millichamp. No doubt a family name; and some rich heri-
tage must have hung on it, for you would not blast an infant
by calling him Millichamp, and without the alternative of
some Tom, Dick or Jabez, unless he were to be bettered

thereby. Died at Davos, poor fellow! Tuberculosis, of course. *Spes phthisica* accounted for everything.

With everything accounted for, Jeremy began to look at Millichamp's works all over again, and more attentively. The lady languidly rejoicing in pink had had her head cut off and stuck on again, for a red band of decollation encircled her neck exactly halfway up—a neat job. The mauve-bearded hermit was fondling a beaver. Welsh saints, all of them, Gwennies and Taffies wringing a hard livelihood out of the rocky, peacock-blue landscape; all of them, except for the beaver, hollow-eyed and haggard. Perhaps they were all self-portraits; but more likely they were influenced by Burne-Jones. Their feet were Burne-Jonesian. Wan.

Jeremy now went into the vestry in pursuit of a stepladder. Stepladders, though extraliturgical, are essential in church furnishing; you can't fasten Christmas holly to lamp brackets without them. There was a stepladder. He carried it into the chancel and mounted it for a nearer view of the east window. It was as he thought. A cartouche in the right-hand corner bore the legend "Poivre et Cie., Bruxelles." Millichamp, devoted to his art, would not have just posted his cartoons to Brussels. He accompanied them, lodging in some modest hotel in the rue Pacheco, going daily to the atelier to watch their sublimation into the fervor and unction of Belgian glass. But he did not leave Brussels without giving a pat to the nose of the dog on the door of the Town Hall. He was an animal lover, as the beaver testified.

Jeremy was still on the stepladder when there was the noise of a door grinding on its hinges. He had not perfectly made up his mind how to account for himself when the grinding of hinges turned into the groaning of a clock going to strike. It was five o'clock. He must hurry back for tea.

At tea, however spiritless the conversation, he would say nothing about Millichamp. When you have accompanied your

wife to rural Carmarthenshire on a mission of mercy, it is better to be thought a doltish, buttered-scone-devouring volup-
tuary than to risk upsetting a hostess who is also a sister-in-law
and a widow in her affliction. Celinda had been sharpening
her affliction by reading her late husband's diaries. They had
thrown her into such a pet that she was now threatening to
have a nervous breakdown. Millichamp might awaken chords.
Chords were twanging off all over the place, which made their
mission of mercy unreposeful and not at all what one expects
of a country visit. In fact, it was Mary's mission; Jeremy had
just come along. His profession—he was a crime-story writer
—did not tie him to London, and he liked being tied to
Mary's apron strings. But even in the privacy of their bedroom
he would not, he decided, talk about Millichamp just yet. In-
cipient stories, like rising dough, must be left in an even tem-
perature under a napkin, and Millichamp was so far no more
than a speculation how a crime might be twisted round a
blameless character and bring it to ruin—it would be fun to
have a comfortless immoral ending for a change. Definitely, he
couldn't expose Millichamp to Mary's approval and have him
rising all to one side. He would just say, if asked, that he had
been looking round the church.

All the same, he could do with knowing a little more.

"What's the name of your parson, Celinda? Have you had
him long?"

"He's a locum tenens—called Pringle. I never expected to
hear Jim buried by a Scotch accent."

"Wasn't it a Colonel Pringle who—" Mary spoke too late.

"But life is full of surprises, isn't it?" Celinda continued
meaningly, and burst into tears.

Anyway, Pringle would be no good: he was a locum, and
knew nothing. If he had been the incumbent, with his family
tree planted on Ben Nevis, one could have questioned him
without putting one's foot in a hornet's nest; whereas every

Welshman is related to every other Welshman, and charged like a pepper pot with family pride—which was going to make research ticklish.

But why hang on Pringles? Millichamp had a blameless character, considerable private means, a rickety talent, a passion to implement it; he was consumptive, fond of animals, an admirer of Burne-Jones, a member of the Church of England. What more could a man want? Jeremy had built up viable figures on less than that. All he had to do was to decide on a crime. Wales was a pastoral country, sadism was In; the crime might be some sort of werewolfery, drinking the hot blood of sheep—an accusation that would be agony to the gentle, animal-loving Millichamp. Perhaps it would be better to make him a poet. It is less trouble to invent bad poetry than to describe bad painting, and poetry would lead him out on midnight walks.

But then again, one mustn't lose sight of the beaver.

Jeremy visited the church next morning, and this time gave particular attention to the pulpit. It had been constructed by the same hand—presumably the estate carpenter's—as the font cover and with the same view of giving Millichamp scope. Each of its five panels had a half-length damozel in profile (Millichamp ran to profiles) whose lips were parted, whose eyes glittered in sunken sockets, whose taper fingers clutched tapers, whose features expressed such weariness and despair that it was obvious the five damozels had unitedly given up hope of the sermon overhead ever coming to an end. It was also obvious that Millichamp had begun on the northernmost damozel and progressed methodically widdershins, the profiles and weariness becoming more emphatic with each repetition, like a Rossini crescendo in a Rossini funeral march—if that various-minded man ever composed one, which, on the law of averages, seemed likely.

The church cleaner had come in soon after Jeremy did. She was now dusting so assiduously beside him that he was forced

to say something, and said, "Good morning." She remarked
that she could see he was looking at the pulpit, and that there
was a story about it.

Jeremy told himself not to get excited, and asked what the
story was.

"It's a celebrated pulpit. There's not another like it in all
Wales. It is called 'The Five Daughters Pulpit.' They were
daughters of the rector, and died, all five of them, of scarlet
fever. You can see they are sisters by the family likeness."

"Do you happen to know who painted it?"

"Everybody knows that. It was their aunt—the week before
they sickened. Providential, really." With that she went off
with her Turk's-head and gave a flick to Millichamp's tablet.
Si monumentum requiris, indeed.

Reflections on the common lot—he, too, had every reasona-
ble expectation of being forgotten—made him so gloomy at
lunch that Celinda, convulsively gulping down barley water,
kept glancing at Mary with commiseration. After lunch, Mary
cornered him and said it was a fine afternoon and he must either lie down or buy her some stamps in Lampeter—otherwise
she would not be answerable.

"Why Lampeter?"

"It's miles away, and you could have tea there."

Jeremy bought the stamps at the Llanyspytty post office.
There he asked the way to Llanyspytty Hen. The postmistress
gave him careful directions and drew a map for him on the
back of a telegraph form, so that he should not be in danger
of missing the turning which went off rather suddenly at the
foot of the one in four hill. Then, carefully looking past him,
she inquired, "Are you a relation?"

From Australia? From California? But probably it would be
wiser to remain just an admirer.

"You'd have to be a relation to be let in. It's a nunnery
where they cure lady dipsomaniacs. Terrible it is what they go
through."

For all that, he set out for Llanyspytty Hen, missed the turning, and drove furiously on toward Aberystwyth. Not that he meant to go to Aberystwyth; but he was resolved not to go to Lampeter. A wasted afternoon, he said to himself; he would have been better employed lying down and finding a suitable crime to wind round Millichamp, or even leading him a trifle astray—the least one could do for the poor chap. A wasted afternoon, even if he had not missed the turning—for why should he feel this craving to visit Millichamp's birthplace? If the story needed a birthplace, a birthplace could be invented; backgrounds were always a pleasure, they afforded more variety than crime. For that matter, why be so fettered to that tablet? Millichamp—his Millichamp—could have been born on the Isle of Wight. It was merely because he did not like being worsted that Jeremy took pains on his way back to spot the turning at the foot of the one in four hill and to hazard his tires along an execrable lane till he saw a rank of calm, smokeless chimney pots, and a high brick wall, and the word "PRIVATE" on a solid wooden gate. He also saw a well-used trail leading through rhododendrons to a tall tree. He got out, and followed it. By climbing the tree as others had done before him he got a raking view of lawns and gravel paths and Millichamp's birthplace. It was decent late Georgian, with a portico. He, Jeremy, could have done with it very nicely. Not so Millichamp. Millichamp would have chafed at it. The sun sank, and Jeremy came down from the tree. His mind was at peace. Though it was now too late to start hunting for other churches Millichamp might have been a benefactor to, this could be done tomorrow, and the next day, and the next day maybe. For now his call was to a Millichamp untouched by crime. It was a monograph he wanted to write.

Thinking of research and dedication and the calm joys of those who write monographs, and the satisfaction of unhorsing reviewers from their preconceived ideas, he returned a changed Jeremy: dreamy, perhaps, and imperfectly attentive, but mild as Celinda's barley water. Asked where he had been, he replied, "Lampeter. A delightful place. It's got so much quality. I must go there again. By the way, Mary, I bought you some stamps there."

A morning light is best, so he set out immediately after breakfast, explaining he would be out for lunch.

"Lampeter again?" said Celinda.

"Probably. But other places too. I feel there's so much to see. By the way, can you lend me a guidebook?"

The guidebook concentrated on castles. What he wanted was a Church of England guidebook. But during the morning he inspected four churches, and after lunch three more. The last of these rewarded him with an early Millichamp—in his scroll manner. The scrolls framed an archway. They were mauve, shaded with green, and writhed from a rhomboidal tablet on which were the words, in Gothic lettering, "I AM THE DOOR."

He had heard of a man in the North of England who signed everything with a mouse. It was a pity that Millichamp had not felt the same way about his beaver. Even a quite formal beaver would be a clue—besides acting as a preservative; for no one, however vandalous, would obliterate a beaver. During the next two days Gilbert came on what he felt almost sure were traces of Millichamp. He felt quite sure about the Royal Arms above the south door of St. Tudoc's, for the lion and the unicorn were by a later hand than the coat of arms, and both were so characteristically elongated, and the lion so wistful, that no beaver was needed. It seemed unlike Millichamp to stay his hand at mere repainting. But the windows were lozenges of red and green glass, the pulpit was Jacobean —nice enough in its way but not what he wanted just then— the reredos was after Murillo, and there was no organ case; they used a harmonium. Jeremy was going away when something impelled him to rip back a corner of the green baize tacked to the back of the instrument. One corner was enough.

Behind the baize was a Millichamp in the artist's best manner, the manner of Llanyspytty. The lady was reclining by a small brook, singing in profile and accompanying herself with a mandolin. An anchor was reclining on the lady. Bulrushes mingled with the arum lilies. Overhead was a thundercloud, its forked lightning playing among the crags.

That evening he was the life and soul of the dinner table, and accounted for it by the sea air he had breathed at Fishguard. He was bursting to tell Mary about the lady of the harmonium, but Millichamp was still too dear a secret to be profaned. Mary was demonstrably managing much better without him. Celinda looked almost affable, and as though she too had a secret enlivening her breast. Indeed, it was she who showed more interest in Fishguard, asking him how it compared with Lampeter.

The next day was a blank. And the next, because it was a Sunday, when churches are infested with congregations. And the next.

On Tuesday the fine weather broke. Celinda condoled with him.

"Yes, it's a bore—because of the light." He stopped himself on the brink.

"Does it make all that difference?" Her voice was positively alert. Mary had certainly done wonders.

Mary now answered for him. "Local color for the next book. Now he'll see it all in a new light. Disillusioning."

This struck him as wantonly provoking chords, and he hurried off to the lady of the harmonium before they twanged.

She was even finer than he remembered; more devotedly, artlessly, sincerely ridiculous. There was an innocence about Millichamp that would touch a brazen heart. Kilvert of the diaries was nothing compared to him—a sophisticated curate of the world. Jeremy intended to make a point of this in the monograph, comparing the romantic, relaxing effect of the Welsh climate on the stranger and on the native son. He was becom-

ing increasingly conscious of the influence of climate—
particularly now that it was raining. Of course, before the in-
ternal-combustion engine, climate must have had an even
greater influence. Millichamp was a child of the Atlantic sea-
board, its visionary gleams, its higher-than-average rainfall.
After the visits to Brussels to stroke the dog's nose, to London
to admire Burne-Jones, he would have returned to his native
climate like a child to its mother's milk. No doubt, he went for
enormous walks, as Kilvert did—but panting for one-dimen-
sional Maggies and Florences with parted lips and languid
subsiding limbs, limbs subsiding like macaroni dropped into
boiling saucepans; for mild mauve-bearded hermits instead of
eccentric clergymen. Artist and benefactor. No doubt his bene-
factions were as idealistically incompetent as his art: drunken
beggars and fraudulent widows. And all to end, poor Millichamp, coughing his lungs up at Davos, tended by sturdy,
red-cheeked Swiss nurses, exposed to full sunlight on a bal-
cony, breathing the cruel dry air, staring at totally uncon-
genial mountains. Jeremy's hands on the wheel twitched to be
typing the monograph. It only remained to find a few more
substantiating examples of Millichamp the artist; Millichamp
the man was already in the bag.

So Jeremy continued to drive about questing for Millichamps, extending his researches into Pembrokeshire, Cardi-
ganshire, and Montgomeryshire. Meanwhile Celinda continued to be all that is kind and tactful to Mary, and to say at
intervals, "Remember, you'll always have *me*."

On Friday, Jeremy reached his reward. It was as though
Millichamp had led him on to it, encouraging him to perse-
vere up the rocky bridle path, to press on among brambles, to
wade through the sopping long grass of the graveyard—and
then to go all the way back to get the church key from Mrs.
Price of Bala Cottage.

It was a large key; it dwarfed the door of the parish church
of St. Gwallior. And then the door stuck.

He forced it open into semidarkness and a smell of paraffin and decay. The east window glowed before him. It was Millichamp at his best, Poivre et Cie. at their most compelling. St. Gwallior must have been one of those saints who navigated in sieves or on millstones, for here he was, in the center lancet, an ascetic figure about ten foot high, with his beard—a rich mulberry shade this time—streaming in the wind, and the stormy billows licking his wan feet. In the right-hand lancet were the green hills of Ireland, in the left the peacock-blue crags of Wales; and a pair of angels in profile floated above them, the one waving him farewell, the other waving him welcome. They must have been conceived about the same date as the supporters of the Royal Arms at St. Tudoc's; there was the same convention of very long tapering bodies and short legs.

Rain beat on the windows. Rain dripped through the roof, and off the black waterproof sheeting draped over the lectern. Moisture glistened on the walls. The nave was thronged with pews, and it seemed to Jeremy he had never seen pews look so positive. He noticed an intermittent light tapping, and looking round discovered it came from a trail of ivy which had squirmed in through a cracked window and wagged to the wind outside. Only then did he see that the walls were thronged with Millichamps; with angels trumpeting, or waving scrolls, or clasping lilies, or hanging head downward to succor, or carrying babes to Heaven, or just flying about on call. Below angel level the scene darkened; incidents in the life of St. Gwallior were taking place—so Jeremy supposed, though the only incident he could feel sure of was an archer shooting at half a gray donkey. The rest was lost in cracks, blotches, running sores of damp rising and leaks trickling, stretches where the plaster had fallen off, areas where penciled nipples and mustaches had been attacked with a scrubbing brush.

Seek no further. He had found the end of his monograph

and the emblem of Millichamp in this desolate church with its ruining murals and its enduring, implacable, glazed testimony to the ludicrous pretensions of his art. Seek no further, delay no longer. He was chilled to the bone and couldn't wait to get back and begin writing it all down.

There was a man standing in the porch when Jeremy let himself out. He turned round, disclosing that he was a clergyman, and said, "Good afternoon."

"Good afternoon," said Jeremy coldly; for at the sight of the clerical collar he was suddenly in a fury at such neglect of Millichamp. "Your church needs repairing."

"Few know that better than I," said the clergyman. "You should attend a service here. We have one every fourth Sunday. You'd bring the congregation up to six. Let me deal with the key. It takes knowing."

Jeremy wished he had begun more politely.

"I'm sorry you found it locked. Mrs. Price told me you had walked back for the key. I came up to ask you in for a drink. You'll need it. It's a bad idea to get chilled on top of getting wet."

He walked ahead, swinging the key. Jeremy followed. At the foot of the bridle path the clergyman turned round, saying formally, "Welcome to my parish."

"But isn't that your church?"

"It's one of them. I have four parishes. But this is the genuine Lateran. Do you mind climbing this wall? We all do. It's the shortcut to the kitchen door."

He sat Jeremy down in a wide kitchen, clean and bare and smelling of gingerbread, and gave him tea laced with rum and a large slice of the newly baked parkin. Indoors, he showed his age; but his gait was limber, and his voice, and his conversation. He talked about depopulation, and with affection about owls. Since he said nothing about his church that needed repairing, Jeremy had to begin.

"Can you tell me anything about Millichamp Howel? I think that's a window of his, in your church—and some remains of wall paintings. I'm interested in him. He seems to be a sort of early mannerist."

"He was my great-aunt. Have another slice."

"Your great-aunt . . . No, thank you."

"I got here too late to save the frescoes. I don't know that I would have saved them, in any case. Have you seen the things at Llanyspytty? She was born there; they couldn't keep her out. After that, she went all over the place. She must have broken the heart of many a bicycle. But she was a kind old Tartar, God rest her soul. She gave me a parrot for Christmas, just before she went off to her winter sporting and broke her neck."

"She broke her neck?"

"At Davos, falling off a bobsled."

"Millichamp is an unusual name," said Jeremy.

"*Mille champs.* It's a family name."

That he should have been right in that one trumpery detail mocked Jeremy's total loss. Millichamp, the companion of his thoughts, the object of his vows, was gone, and the monograph with him. He would just have to write another bloody crime story. It was all he was good for. It was all anybody wanted of him, and they didn't want it much.

As he drove into Llanyspytty he saw the church lighted up. Mary had said something about not being late because Celinda thought of going to the choir practice. No wonder Celinda had perked up so, with Mary devoting all her attention to her. If Mary had asked him not to be late because by seven she would be thinking of road accidents, it would not now be quarter past eight. Celinda's car was in the garage. They were in the sitting room, waiting for him. When he entered, muddied, morose, and smelling of rum, Mary gave him one glance, and the air one sniff. Her face wrinkled, her eyes narrowed to slits, and she turned away to hide her feelings. Even so, her shoulders heaved, and at intervals during dinner she uncontrollably giggled. Jeremy was glad to see her so merry. He would not have been merry if he had spent a day with Celinda while Mary was out gallivanting to unknown destinations—but the sexes are no guide to each other. She had a delightful giggle, he was glad to see her merry, he was also glad he had not told her about Millichamp. It is better to grieve alone.

But a man in his sister-in-law's house cannot hope to grieve alone. His grief (particularly if he is catching a cold and every sneeze is remarked on) requires an amplitude of anonymity, a detachment from domestic trivialities. It requires a club. On Sunday evening Jeremy said he must go back to town, to read up about barratry in the London Library. He would catch the early train, leaving the car at the station for Mary to pick up later. He would stay at his club.

When they had seen him off, Mary and Celinda took a turn round the garden. Mary commented on the clearing skies and the robin's autumn song. "Look, Celinda! There he is. He's killed his father and can eat worms with a quiet mind."

Celinda said that nature was basically cruel.

"I don't know about that. Taken on the whole, I think nature is rather nice."

"Not human nature."

Mary whistled to the robin, then asked when Celinda's twins were coming home from their boarding school.

"You've asked that at least fifty times, Mary. Not that I blame you. I think you are heroic. I suppose it's better to know at the time—at least you're spared the shock. But say it I must, I've never seen anything so blatant. It almost reconciled me to Jim, for at least he had the decency not to brandish his horrid affairs."

"Poor Jim—I mean poor Jeremy!"

"Practically the moment he got here. And then saying he'd brought you back some stamps. Stamps, indeed! From Lampeter! As if he couldn't have bought them at the post office. And then thinking he'd throw you off the scent by talking about Fishguard."

"I suppose one might go to Fishguard, if one wanted to look at the sea."

"Wanted to look at the sea! It wasn't the sea Jeremy wanted just then. He wanted something very different. And got it, too. Don't you remember, that was the evening when he came back smirking like a cat from the larder? My heart bleeds for you, Mary. I can't think why you take it so calmly."

"Jeremy says I always take things calmly."

"More than he does. *What* a state he was in when he came back on Friday! I suppose they'd got drunk and quarreled. Mary, I can't bear to see you treated like this; and in my house, too. What does Jeremy think I am? A springboard for Lampeter?"

"I'm sorry you've been so upset, Celinda."

"Upset? I've been in agonies."

"But if you had asked me, I could have put you out of your agonies; I could have told you it wouldn't last, this Lampeter person. Jeremy's serious mistress lives in London."

Oh, poor Jeremy, thrown to the wolves! But really it had been irresistible. Besides, she would now be able to return with a clear conscience, leaving a happy, satisfied Celinda. Celinda wouldn't think any the worse of Jeremy—in fact, she'd think the better of him. She'd soon be making handsome allowances for him, married to that cynical, cold-blooded, and —one must admit—by now quite unattractive wife. So Celinda, rosy as a ghoul, would forget her own misfortunes in feeding on Mary's, and by tomorrow night Mary would be telling Jeremy how he had been thrown to the wolves—a confidence to which she hoped he would respond by telling her what he had been up to and where he had been to catch that shocking cold. She must remember to buy some lemons on the journey back. Jeremy's old-fashioned colds always responded to hot lemon and sal volatile.

THE PERFECT SETTING

Waking, Adolphine Corbett saw the fathomless blue of a summer morning; and remembered it was Thursday and that Hudson was coming that afternoon, bringing a Mr. Bannerman, who was interested in Oswald.

It was not to be looked for that Hudson would bring anybody who was interested in Oswald Corbett's widow. Those who came on her account (there were fewer and fewer of them) came unbrought, and came (it is the way of the aging) to demand interest and not to display it, beyond a few inquiries about her health. It should have interested them; it was so uncommonly good. But they preferred to dwell on their inferior own.

Oswald had died fifteen years ago, aged sixty-seven, but was still interesting because he was a poet. If you can once make a name as a poet people will go on being interested in you for quite a time after your death, if only because you have succeeded in doing so—a rare feat and interesting in itself to people who otherwise feel no interest in poetry. Because of Oswald, she would shortly meet Mr. Bannerman. Because of Oswald, she still had Hudson. When he and Dinah divorced, it was Hudson Moberley who remained, more of a son-in-law than ever, devoted, assiduous, bringing people who were interested in Oswald. There had been Mr. O'Flaherty, who unstemmably quoted poem after poem, and Mrs. Bugler, who went through the manuscripts examining every watermark, and took so long about it that Dinah seized on her as a pretext for wanting a divorce, and Father Garment, S.J., who traced a latent Catholicism in Oswald's "Three Odes to Ovid," and Professor Mackenzie, who translated them into Lallans. There had been admirers from America, some writing poetry themselves, others theses, and from Japan, who hissed, and from Australia and the Philippines, to whom he had been an inspiration; and an enormous young man from Tiflis, who came by mistake—what he wanted was Cobbett—but was charming and particularly admired the door scraper. There were people who came with cameras. There was the woman with a tape recorder, who sat for hours in the garden waiting to record the owls. Of late years, there had not been quite so many of them. But now Hudson had dredged up this Bannerman, and she would have to go through it all over again.

The library. The manuscripts: the early ones, dashed down on odds and ends of paper in the delicate sharp handwriting like bird footprints on snow; the later group, when he was using India ink, blackened with scratchings out, clotted with alternatives, the delicate opinionated calligraphy grown hectoring. The portraits, the first publications, the Poetry Bookshop broadsheets; the shelf of folios and the splendid Ovid on the lectern; the foot muff and the stuffed eagle owl and the coffeepot. Tea in the dining room. After tea, the garden: the screen of aspen poplars, the pleached alley, the mulberry, crouched and dwarfish with age, the fountain. In the garden people would exclaim, "The perfect setting!" or, "You'd never think you were so close to London!" Some said both.

At this point Hudson would give her her due as a perfect setting herself, telling how she found the house, long derelict, its garden a mass of nettles and willow herb, a resort of truant children, owls, and cats, and knew at once that it was the house for Oswald Corbett.

"You did not even consult him, did you?"

"No, Hudson. I never bothered him with things like that. I just bought it, and when it was restored and the garden put in order I gave it to him as a surprise."

This made it clear that the money was hers, and left Oswald's aloofness unblemished. It also deterred inquiries as to what he had meant in such and such a passage—though such inquiries were things of the past, since Oswald's admirers had for some time known exactly what he meant.

She did not say—and Hudson could not, since she had never told him—that Adolphine Ezra, idling among her riches, had bought Trafalgar Lodge when she had met Oswald Corbett exactly once and not particularly liked him, but was so much under the spell of his poetry that to fit him with a dwelling to match it seemed a very natural thing to do, regardless of how he was to be got there. With the artlessness of wealth, she had not stopped to think that the dwelling presupposed enough money to live in it. This difficulty did not arise. When they met again, she liked him better. The fountain had not begun to play, the electricians were still in the house, when with the calm acceptance of total astonishment she heard him ask her to marry him. It was not what she had meant. Later on, she sometimes regretted the frustration of her first simple design. But it would not have done. Oswald could never have lived in Trafalgar Lodge without someone to run it, and to look after Dinah, his pretty little bastard.

Hudson, embodiment of contented mental penury, was a poor exchange for Dinah. She did not suppose that she would be much enriched by Bannerman. She looked away from the blue summer sky and the tremor of light on the aspens, and contemplated the telephone by her bedside. She could put them off and have another day to herself. Almost all her days were such, but as one grows old one increasingly values them. But in this bed Oswald had lain dying, angrily stoical, telling her not to be a fool and cursing the weekly in which his last volume had been reviewed among the also-rans. Hudson must come. Louise must bake her lemon biscuits, speciality of the house.

Hudson came, slightly out of breath as though he had brought Mr. Bannerman in his jaws. He had put on his summer waistcoat and wore a carnation in his buttonhole. Mr. Bannerman wore no waistcoat. He had a purposeful look—as though he had come about the plumbing.

"How do you do?"

"Oh. Er. How do you do?" He seemed startled by the inquiry.

Hudson got rid of the silence by asking if they could see the library. She opened the door, and stood back for Hudson to do his piece. Disregarding him, Mr. Bannerman exclaimed, "I say, that's rather remarkable," and went straight for the eagle owl. "Tell me about this. What sort of bird is it? Did he shoot it? I didn't know he went in for that sort of thing."

Hudson said it was an eagle owl, and that in life its eyes would have been an even brighter flame color. The French name for it was *un grand-duc.* Perhaps Bannerman remembered that Rostand had included a *grand-duc* in "Chantecler." Mr. Bannerman briefly shook his head, and continued to stare at the owl, which, naturally, continued to stare back.

"But he didn't shoot it," she said. "As far as I know, he never shot anything. He certainly wouldn't have shot an owl. He was particularly fond of them."

Hudson helpfully murmured the owl stanza from the second ode to Ovid: " 'Roofed by your chuckling pibroch, your cries of rapine, I neither rustic nor innocent snore the merrier. . . .' How many variants of that last line, Adolphine?"

She opened the boulle cabinet holding the manuscripts. Hudson followed her. Mr. Bannerman did not turn.

"I believe you are hypnotized by that bird," remarked Hudson playfully.

"I was thinking about it as a jacket," said Mr. Bannerman. "It would have to come out of its glass shade, of course."

Hudson caught back a cry of delight. His dull good face was transfigured by servile triumph, and he gave her a quick little nod. If the best he could bring in was an ornithologist, and a hack one at that . . . The glass shade should never be lifted off Oswald's owl for a bird book. Then she heard Hudson say, "Mr. Bannerman is thinking of writing a book about Oswald."

"Not too fast, Moberley. Not too fast. I am a professional writer"—Mr. Bannerman sat down at Oswald's writing table —"and I don't like to take a thing on unless I can feel reasonably sure I can do it adequately, and that there will be a public for it. And a publisher. You may not know, Mrs. Corbett, but since your husband's time the cost of bringing out a book has more than trebled. If you are by way of buying books—"

"I buy them from time to time."

"Then you will realize how the whole picture has changed."

"More misprints."

Hudson, poor wretch, was twiddling in agony. His lower lip drooped, and he goggled.

Mr. Bannerman continued, "Now, Moberley has been at me for a long time to do a book about your husband—he's not pre-empted, I take it? Well, it's a shot in the dark, but it appeals to me. That early-twentieth-century background, you know. It's a vanished age—and practically untouched. Men of letters. Bohemians. The Poetry Bookshop. The discovery of Cornwall. Rosicrucians. Was your husband a Rosicrucian?"

"Not that I know of."

"Well, he'd have met them."

"He wasn't at all gregarious."

"Oh. A solitary." Mr. Bannerman's face fell. The plumbing wasn't as straightforward as he had assumed. He brooded.

Hudson remarked that in 1912 Oswald went to Bayreuth. Mr. Bannerman's silence rejected this. If I go on being patiently disagreeable, she thought, he'll go away and write about Aleister Crowley.

"A solitary? . . . A solitary? . . . Why, of course, that owl!
It's a gift. I felt it, the instant I came into this room. I can
build up that owl into something terrific—Poe's raven will be
nothing to it. It's exactly what I want. It's a gift. I say, Moberley, you might copy out those grand duke bits. They'd all
help to build it up. Did he have it from a child, Mrs. Corbett?"

"No. He bought it in 1933, at Pitlochry."

"Exactly. Ex-actly! And it was in the middle thirties, wasn't
it, that he changed his style and began to write those abstruse
poems? Black poems. And went off on the classics."

It was as if Hudson had brought in a very cheap
Mephistopheles—a self-winding Mephistopheles with an inex-
haustible mechanism, enabling it to dart at false conclusions, to
rebound from obstacles of fact. So it wasn't surprising if this
fatuous importee should momentarily, accidentally, hit on
something which might seem of significance. There sat Hudson beaming with collaboration. But what was this dizzied
weakening in herself as though she too were under the fascina-
tion of a vulgar mind?

"And this is where it all happened," said Bannerman, giving
a brisk glance round the room. "Of course, it's a wonderful
setting. I really feel as if I could write poems myself in a room
like this."

"Only he didn't write them here," she said. "He wrote in
hotel bedrooms. He used to go to some industrial town, like
Retford or Wellingborough or Wolverhampton, and take a
room at a commercial hotel or a railway hotel, and write
there."

"Oh, thank you, thank you!" Mr. Bannerman sprang up
and seized her hand. "This is tremendous! I had no idea of it.
Moberley never told me."

"He didn't know."

Mr. Bannerman was now pumping Hudson's hand. "It's so
right, it's out of this world. Wellingborough! Wolverhampton!
Commercial hotels! Moberley, isn't this marvelous? It's like a

blood transfusion. I knew I could do a lot with the owl, but it would have been a bit literary, a bit too much in the past. This brings him to life, makes a vital figure of him. There'll be a public for his poems again or I don't know the book market. Wolverhampton!"

"Yes, Bannerman, you're right. I'm sure you're right. My father-in-law will be read with new eyes. And that's what matters."

"That's what matters. By the way"—Mr. Bannerman's voice tautened—"it's an understood thing, isn't it, that we keep these commercial hotels strictly under our hats?"

"And the owl?" she asked.

"The owl too, of course."

Tea was quickly disposed of. Mr. Bannerman couldn't wait to get back and start on the book. Hudson, making a creditable recovery, told her between two slices of cake that she had kept the best wine to the last. Nothing was said of the garden.

When she had waved them off she returned to the library and closed the boulle cabinet. Nothing turns out as one meant. Perhaps by that one exasperated disclosure she had at long last done something for Oswald's poetry. It didn't seem likely, but conceivably it was possible.

THE GREEN TORSO

"Then there's Hilldrop Crescent," mused Mr. Partridge, who had been expatiating on northern London's richness in murders. "The Crippens. She was Belle Elmore, a variety artist— but of course you know that. Nothing like being murdered to keep your memory green." He saddened his voice. "But the people in entertainment who don't get murdered, nobody remembers them. When one grows old one becomes a compendium of forgotten artists. God knows, it's no pleasure being a creaking octogenarian, but I sometimes feel a positive obligation to stay alive because of these poor quaint ghosts who will vanish with me."

Ronald Pim wrote down "creaking octogenarian"—but unobtrusively. Though Mr. Partridge's replying letter had shown a prompt readiness to be interviewed, his manner now implied that he was putting up with an indignity.

"Have you never thought of writing—"

While Ronald was hesitating between "your memoirs" and "your autobiography," Mr. Partridge had decided to go on. "There was a fellow at the Coliseum who bicycled round and round. You mightn't think there was much in that. There was everything. He wore a rusty black suit, his face was dead white, his bicycle was ruinous. He rode it round and round, very slowly, in smaller and smaller circles. When it seemed that it was bound to fall inward, he would twitch it upright and go circling on with an expression of fixed despair. At the end of his turn he would ride off into the wings. And the rear tire would come loose and thwack his bottom. All gone. All gone."

"I've heard about him," exclaimed Ronald Pim. "From my grandmother. His name was O'Donoghue."

"It was nothing of the sort," said Mr. Partridge furiously. After a pause he resumed with arrogant patience. "Then there was Vera Valetta. She was in pantomime—a Principal Boy. She wore a top hat tilted over one eye and sang patriotic songs. She weighed twelve stone, she had a tiny waist, splendid legs. A regular Edward VII type. Then she vanished into the Midlands and when she came back she did the Widow Twanky line for a year or two. But her weight got too much for her, her splendid legs ulcerated; finally one of them had to be cut off."

"Poor thing!"

"Ha-ha-ha! That wasn't the end of it. She had it embalmed, kept it in her bedroom. And during the blitz—she lived on into the blitz—when she was carried down to the shelter the leg had to be brought too."

He looked at his watch and remarked that it was time for his bread and milk.

After leaving the ground-floor flat in Canonbury, Ronald could not disabuse himself of the notion that Mr. Partridge, preserving more than a memory of Vera Valetta, kept her leg in a drawer of his desk and gnawed at it when alone. Such fancies are best shaken off by exercise. He would make his way back to Paddington on foot. He knew his way about London.

When he began working as a draftsman in the firm of Loudon Johnston, Architects and Structural Engineers, Ronald lived with his mother in Tonbridge and commuted. While his fellow travelers were reading their daily papers he stared out at the stratification of the landscape: the fields and orchards yielding to ruralized housing estates, the first urban phenomenon of cemeteries, remnants of stately Victorian domesticity holding out like redoubts among factories and shopping centers; then the sudden darkening and densification of the older London, brandishing nineteenth-century church spires, clutching a single pear or apple tree in a back garden; then the postwar territory of bombed sites and Bauhaus blocks of flats and the spaced-out glassy towers of commercial skyscrapers, rising here, risen there, some of particular interest since they were the achievements of Loudon & Johnston. Persisting among them, huddled together, low on the ground, were the original streets and terraces of artisans' dwellings, brick-built, with their erected hackle of chimneys and crooked chimney pots. As these became daily more familiar to him they simultaneously became more remote. It was as though they were the vestigial fauna of London, wearing the protective coloration of their native clay and soon to be wiped out. And then he saw the cranes along the river and the ugly majesty of Tower Bridge.

His mother died. He moved to London. The firm, esteeming him as a reliable worker, pitying him too for his facial deformity, and judging he could not say boo to a goose, found lodgings for him in Paddington with a Mrs. Palmer, the widow of one of their lorry drivers. When Palmer's workmate, who kept a friendly eye on the widow, asked what the new lodger was like, she replied that you couldn't wish for anyone quieter—a bit of an old maid, in fact; but with a horrible birthmark like that it wasn't to be wondered at if he kept himself to himself.

The birthmark was a port-wine stain, covering Ronald Pim's right cheek and extending over both his eyes, so that he seemed to be peering out through the eyeholes of a mask. It was his mother's sighs that first made him aware of it; they imposed a sense of guilt on him which he could not shake off, even when his school friends (at that time he could still make friends quite easily) countered it with cheerful ribaldry, pretending that they could foretell the weather by his change of hue, calling him Old Port and Starboard and supposing that when he was older he would be put to use as a traffic signal. By the time his mother died, he had given up all thought of friends. He was a monstrosity. He must keep out of people's way and any friendliness surviving in him be given to things.

But London was too large to notice him; he could make a friend of London. He bought books about it: about the City and its churches, about the Thames and its bridges, about Westminster and Mayfair and Old Chelsea. He bought them in second-hand shops and off barrows, read them attentively, did as they bid—unless what they bade him admire had been done away with by war or progress or the Ecclesiastical Commissioners. But it was a stranger's London they told of. He did not care to be reminded that he was a stranger there himself. It was only from Victorian compilations, proudly expatiating on the sewage system, the docks and the vast quantities of merchandise they handled, the improvements in public lighting, Guy's Hospital, the Blackwall Tunnel, Spurgeon's Tabernacle that he got a sense of reality, of an intricate metropolitan existence, of a population who lived and worked and had their vivid present in that obscure past, and had an inherited past of their own. "As black as old Newgate," he heard a woman at a bus stop say. She had not the smallest idea what she was talking about, and London spoke through her. He went on collecting books, and from time to time some chance dull fact—the acreage of a cattle market, the statistics of a fever hospital—would drop a seed in his mind. But the books all had the same failing: they left off where his curiosity began. The darkening and densification he had looked down on from the railway track, the agglutination of what had once been outskirts—parishes, villages, hamlets—into that enormous, close-packed region encircling the London of the guidebooks and the histories, they dismissed as "The East End," "South of the River," "North of the Terminuses."

There was nothing for it but to go and see for himself.

Place names remained, and some of them, like Balham and Tooting, were laughable and some, like Isle of Dogs, were alarming. The sinister names, though, were those of districts so featureless—not even distinguished by a prison or a legend of violence—and so numerous that one did not know where they were, whether they lay north or south of the river: Homerton, Kingsland, Dalston, Newington, Stockwell, Plaistow, Walworth, Old Ford. The London Atlas knew them and recorded, in brown, every Ada Street, Albert Street, Dahomey Road, Bateman's Road, Railway Terrace, Chapel Lane, Gunn Square, Blackadder's Rents of their intricate, compressed intestines. And in the evenings he laid the Atlas open beside his supper tray and tried to memorize a route. He was afraid to carry the Atlas with him; it would proclaim him a stranger, and his face was proclamatory enough.

Sunday morning—the earlier the better, when there were only a few communicants abroad—was the best time to set out. Mrs. Palmer, requested to prepare egg sandwiches and a thermos of tea the night before, decided Mr. Pim had got religion. So in a way he had: a missionary's call to go forth and reclaim some portion of the unknown, to ascertain something in the physiognomy of De Beauvoir Town which distinguished it from Kentish Town or Camden Town. Whenever possible, he traveled by subway. A subway has more anonymity, and provides a purer first impression. It was exciting to surface and look round on the unforetellable aspect of a familiar name—the statue of a good public character, perhaps, a sideways view of a churchyard's greenery, a street market in full swing. Street markets released him from his self-consciousness. The vendors saw him as a buyer; the buyers were absorbed in buying.

What could be eaten off a barrow was part of a distinguishing physiognomy. Deptford and New Cross excelled at cockles in spiced vinegar. The same day he made the cockle discovery, standing in the sun with a brisk upriver wind flapping the pa-per-moss flounces on the barrows, he went homeward along the south bank. The bells of St. Paul's and the City churches were ringing for evensong and the sound came airily across the water. It was as much part of a locality as the cockles, and that day he felt he knew London as a friend.

If he had had the moral courage to say boo to his circum-stances he would have left his lodgings in Paddington and moved to southeast London. It had a charm for him because of those staring journeys during which it became familiar yet kept the poetry of being unvisited. But he did not want to hurt Mrs. Palmer's feelings; he would be sorry to give up his evening strolls along the Regent's Canal; there is much to be said for living in a place which casts no spell over you and does you no harm. The spell of continuity had been cast; he did not uproot. The London Atlas was laid open on the same table, the thermos and the egg sandwiches, always tasting just the same, were placed beside it, though now Mrs. Palmer had given up the hypothesis that his Sunday outings were devo-tional. The state of his shoes when he got back was not com-patible. Mud, yes; but not fish scales.

Mrs. Palmer was a Londoner but nothing to Ronald's pur-pose. Like the books which left off where his curiosity began, she was restricted: in her case, to the Royal Family. But one evening when he looked up from the Atlas and noticed that she seemed to be taking an interest in it, he asked her if she knew anything about Hoxton. "Hoxton, Mr. Pim? You aren't thinking of going there, surely?"

It had been a mistake to invoke her. She had never been to Hoxton, could not conceive wishing to go there, had nothing to contribute to the subject. But her repudiation of it dogged his explorings. He could find no physiognomy, no whet, no clue. He walked about aimlessly, eyed by dirty windows, star-tled by bursts of music from transistors. Because he could make nothing of Hoxton he began to feel he had no right to be there, and avoided going there again. His purpose to explore northeast London remained, but an element of duty had come into it; he knew in his heart he was not enjoying himself, and that, if it had not been for Pentonville and one or two burial grounds and the Bedlamite assertion of pre-London in the Hackney Marsh, he might as well have studied it in the Atlas. It was like traversing an index to a book he would never be able to read. And there was so much of it. Beyond the Hackney Marsh it began again and floundered on, the vestigial fauna which would be exterminated under new housing estates, new factories, towers, and boulevards. He could never learn it all and what he had learned was continually being filched from him. A row of small neighborhood shops vanished behind a hoarding and a notice appeared that a bingo hall would be opening shortly; the composure of a once genteel little square was put out of countenance by an eight-story office block. Realizing that he must submit his ambition to his limitations, he turned back to the London south of the Thames. He felt he knew that pretty well till Stevenson, who worked in the same room as he, exclaimed, "Do you mean to say you've never been to The Oval?"

The inquiry (it was made on his thirty-fourth birthday) was not quite so demolishing as it would have been a few years earlier. Ronald had already formed a new ambition.

It began during a conversation with a flower seller outside Kensal Green Cemetery, in the course of which the flower seller remarked that London was not what it was. Ronald was about to reply that he supposed not when the flower seller continued, "You should hear my great-grandfather talk about it in the old days. Why, when he was a kid he used to be taken to Clapton Downs to smell the sea air. And gorged himself for sixpence in the strawberry gardens in East Ham. Cockfighting, donkey races, girls chucking themselves off the bridges—London was more like London then."

"How old is your great-grandfather?"

"Nearer a hundred than ninety. He was a street hawker, used to sell groundsel for canaries, and wild flowers, and bulrushes. Fetched it in from Essex, mostly. He'd walk twenty miles before breakfast and think nothing of it. But he's retired now. His legs are as good as ever but his sight isn't what it was."

"Does he live with you?"

"Wouldn't hear of it. He's got a room off the Whitechapel Road and does everything for himself, shopping and all. You ought to meet him."

The room off the Whitechapel Road glowed with ornaments: fairground vases, statuettes on brackets, plumes of dyed pampas grass, tinny trophies of immortelles, souvenirs of two wars. The old man was himself like a trophy of immortelles. His bald head, his paled blue eyes, his lively cheeks had a tinning of old age on them. His talk was a practiced recital, glowing with violence, exploits, and wonders. He despised the present world because nobody with any cleverness was left in it. That evening, Ronald put a sheet of paper into his typewriter, headed it "A London Character," and described the visit. It came easily to him. Casting about for another London character, he remembered the limping woman who walked by the Regent's Canal. In the past he had eluded conversation with her; now when he wanted it, she wasn't there. But she reappeared, and her absence supplied a pretext. "I haven't seen you here lately." She explained that she had been watching a family of owls who had their nest in the goods yard of Paddington Station. She answered his astonishment by telling him that birds of prey resorted to goods yards for the rats and mice they found there. If she had gone there to find her own provision, she could not have been more matter-of-fact. This London character also lived alone. She worked as a dressmaker and had been watching birds for many years. Some of her identification had been reported in an ornithological journal.

She also went into the typewriter. She was not so easy to write about, for she had not polished her material, but he got her down in the end. Talking to a woman at dusk, listening to the nonagenarian whose sight wasn't what it used to be, had emboldened him to search for more London characters. He discovered that people with something to tell resembled people with something to sell, and that in such a traffic his birthmark could be discounted. When he had finished half a dozen articles, he began to think of seeing them in print. There was a Miss Ewing, Typist & Literary Agent, whose window placard he saw on his way to work. It was an effort to ring her bell, a greater effort to remain on her doorstep. After administering the first shock and seeing how bravely she fixed her hare's eyes on his face, he felt as if she were some small animal he was trying to persuade into a sense of security. It struck him she could not do a great deal of business. Her room was shabby and *The Mill on the Floss* lay open beside her typewriter. To read his articles—the term she used was "to glance over them"—she put on a pair of large spectacles.

Still wearing the spectacles, she told him that she thought she could place his articles in provincial papers—there was, for instance, the *Clackmannan Messenger,* a religious weekly, which liked to put in something about London from time to time—but that first of all the articles must be retyped, with shorter paragraphs and double spacing. She offered to show him how, but he said he would rather she did it. The *Clackmannan Messenger* was a come-down. He had hoped for the *Spectator.* Meanwhile Miss Ewing was saying how much she liked his sketches, especially the retired groundsel seller. "You must write about more queer people like that."

"If I can find them."

"What about Waterloo Station? I'm sure you'd find that a happy hunting ground."

"Waterloo Station?"

"Yes. Where the vagrants and down-and-outs spend the night. You must go there. I'm sure you'd find just the material you want. Some of them have had most interesting lives, you know."

He thanked her and left her—a man charged with a new destiny.

But at the time, he was piqued at learning that Waterloo Station, like The Oval, was an aspect of the London across the river which other people knew about and he did not, and decided that he would find his own routes to London characters. In any case, it was the end of July, his fortnight's holiday was due, and he was, as usual, going to stay with his sister Mattie. This year it was not quite as usual: Mattie had rented a furnished bungalow in Radnorshire, so that the children could have some pony riding. The bookshelf over his bed held several volumes by Arthur Machen—as he understood, a Welsh author. But mixed with evocations of Gwent and Caerleon there were evocations of Pentonville and Clerkenwell and Barnsbury, recalled with the same plangent *hwl*, that lift and lilt of the preacher's voice. Machen, young and solitary, had explored where he, Ronald Pim, had explored; and with a wider experience of unknowable London, for Machen had penetrated to Acton. Unfortunately, Machen was dead. There must be others of his kind, solitary dedicated Londoners: not many of them left but still some; more hermetical than the goods-yard owls but still taking their silent flights. He hurried back to London and spent the remainder of his holiday in bookshops and public libraries, pulling out volume after volume from cases labeled "Autobiographies," "Reminiscences," "Miscellanies." In a bound-up volume of the *London Mercury* for 1931 he found Mr. Partridge, picking holes in Norman Douglas's *London Street Games,* and from the Postal Directory discovered he was still alive, with an address in north London. He had the letter to Mr. Partridge in his pocket on the night he went to Waterloo Station, but it was not posted till late next day—for everything had been scattered out of his head by the horrible solicitations of an old woman who pawed at his fly and said she would be a mother to him. Two nights later, drawn back against his will to that limbo of no departures, he met Marco Brown.

It was the austerity of a musical note, piercing the mumbling and shuffling and coughing as if it were the only valid existence there, which announced him. A guitar; a desultory hand plucking a chord; another chord; a swift flourish; then silence. "It's that Marco and his lot," a voice said. The fitful disembodied music continued, went farther away, returned. The guitar player was walking about. A ringleted golden head moved briefly into a shaft of light, seeming to float in the air. Ronald held out his cigarette case to a man close by him. "Is that Marco?"

The man took a cigarette, stuffed it into a pocket, pointed to his ears. He was deaf. The guitar player struck up more purposefully, playing a tune. People began to hum. Then a tattered high tenor voice took up the tune, wavered, broke off, began again in another key. The guitar player shifted to the singer's key and coaxed him along, thrumming on the strings to fill up where the singer's breath failed. Shouts encouraged them, hands clapped the rhythm. Skirting round sitters and sleepers, Ronald edged his way toward the music. The singer gasped for breath, the guitar thrummed like an animal growling. With a screech the singer hurled himself into another verse and another key, and the guitar hunted him on, and the handclaps closed round him. Willy-nilly, Ronald, standing behind the guitar player, began to clap too. The player turned and took a quick look at him, the ringlets swaying like a curtain. With the movement there was a waft of some very sophisticated perfume. Jesus, thought Ronald—a Jesus by Leonardo; for though it was so dusky and the face only momentarily seen, the identification was compulsive: the golden ringlets and the smooth cheeks, the vaguely smiling mouth and the narrow oval of the chin. Jesus amid his disciples, ministering to the poor and outcast.

The guitar finished off the singer with a loud twanging chord; a last trickle of song came from the open mouth. "Lovely job, man, lovely job," said a disciple, and another said something about ought to be in opera. Jesus was already walking away, laughing and talking as he went. No doubt Jesus among the outcasts also cracked blue jokes. Farther away other voices were gathering. Jesus noosed "Star of the Sea" from the baying medley of tunes, shook it into a quicker measure, syncopated it, commanded it into a chorus, heartfelt and appalling. And again he moved away, and the chorus disintegrated and collapsed.

The first daylight drifted in. It was possible to study the sleeping shapes, clotted together like the debris on a beach after a storm. They slept more resolutely now, as if they knew less time was left to them. A feeling far beyond pity overwhelmed Ronald. His mind had no words left in it. He had lost all curiosity, all interest; he was dragged into a stony assent. The guitar player was at it again—distant, a mosquito noise. Why sting these unfortunates into wakefulness and fever and personality? Let be, let be! He was still standing there when the guitar suddenly twanged at his elbow. He realized that he was being played at. "Why do you come here?" he demanded.

"To give them a chance to show off. It's what we all want, isn't it?" The voice was cool and rational. "Come and have breakfast," it continued.

Breakfasting with Marco and the disciples, swallowing the all-night café's hot sweet coffee and violently flavored meat pies, Ronald was in a stupor of excitement. These were the new young, the inaccessible teen-agers, whom magistrates scolded, whom journalists wrote up, whom traders toadied and dope peddlers beset, whom social experts accounted for, whom everyone was incited to gape at, reprobate, romanticize, whom no one could bring to heel. And here he sat, being talked to as an equal by those who were half his age and did not know his name. Inattentively, he heard himself inviting them to visit him that evening. Unbelievingly, he heard them one and all accepting the invitation, Marco adding, "I can only eat coarse food." He spent his luncheon break buying salami and beer and pickled onions and chocolate biscuits and wondering if he could raise enough chairs for the disciples. He had forgotten to count them.

They came at half past ten, when he had given up hope and could not look Mrs. Palmer in the face. The disciples were not so many as he supposed—a bearded pair who said, "We are Ginger and Pickles," a stocky, red-faced youth with a disproportionately large head and a crew cut (all the others had flowing locks) who didn't speak and was addressed as Stewart, an extremely thin youth wearing a voluminous poncho, and Jessamy, who was from the Midlands and had brought his pet snake in a little hamper. Marco's first words were to demand a saucerful of milk for it. The snake was poured out of its hamper. It seemed languid, and everyone looked at it with concern. Marco began to talk about the difficulty of keeping snakes in artificial conditions: Jessamy's basement was damp.

"I got it a sunray lamp," Jessamy said.

"You ought to get it some rocks—and some heather," said Marco. "If you bought some potted heather and arranged the rocks round the pots, with crevices for it wriggle through, and made it a bathing pool—a large shallow baking tin would do —and ran a constant small trickle of water into it by a pipe from the tap—snakes must have fresh water to bathe in, they are exceedingly cleanly—and had a large bath towel, a gigantic bath towel, to absorb the overflow, your snake would be happier. You could bring down a load of its native rocks from the Pennines."

"Yes, that's all very fine, man, but how am I to practice my ballet steps with rocks all over the floor?"

"You could practice arm movements. Classical Indian dancing concentrates on control of the arm from shoulder to fingertip. I know a waiter in an Indian restaurant who would be delighted to give you lessons. You could learn some of the ragas at the same time. We are all much too insular."

Not once did Marco's vaguely smiling mouth distort itself in a laugh. His voice remained at the same pitch, he showed no elation at his inventiveness, his unanswerable logic, his encyclopedic capacity to discourse on any question and know something unexpected about every subject. He had not an atom of brag or an atom of modesty. It was as though some divine computer were speaking. Or was he more like a snake charmer, at whose piping cobras rose out of earthen vessels and showed their undulating paces? For it had to be admitted that, with the exception of the youth in the poncho, Marco's disciples were an unoriginating lot and depended on him for their animation. Only the grass snake remained indifferent. Only the youth in the poncho was spontaneously dissident and gave a flashing tirade in favor of insularity, during the course of which he made use of half a dozen foreign languages and wanted the nationalists of the world to unite. He was in an anguish of disagreement with everybody, especially Marco, and his pop eyes besought Marco's attention. Marco's attention was as selective and compelling as his guitar playing. Remembering those words "a chance to show off," and habitually aware that his only social hope was to lurk behind his birthmark, Ronald nevertheless began to show off: not the *Clackmannan Messenger,* which would never do in this gathering, but his knowledge of London. Marco listened absorbedly, thrummed him on when he faltered, and at the close told him of three things he must on no account miss, all within a five-minute walk, and exactly how to get to them. One was in a bakery, and he must buy a doughcake (the baker's specialty) and lead the conversation round to healing wells. "It's not enough to trudge along pavements. Use your intuition, snuff the air, and whenever instinct tells you there's something particular, go into the nearest shabby shop and get talking. And always look into shopwindows. That's how Stewart found his peruke. It was in a greengrocer's, with a cat sleeping on it."

"That's right," said the red-faced youth, speaking almost for the first time. "Just what I wanted. I'm a sociologist."

About two in the morning, the snake was returned to its hamper and the party left, saying they would come again on Monday.

Severed from Marco's spell, Ronald did not feel sanguine about his powers to develop conversations with shopkeepers, and did nothing about this; but on his way back from Mr. Prothero he remembered about looking into shopwindows. It was surprising how many of them contained displays of wallpaper. One would think a fever of redecoration was sweeping through the London north of the terminuses if so much of the wallpaper had not been flyblown. In Camden Town he paused by a trayful of books outside a second-hand furniture shop. Among the paperbacks were some solid, dingy volumes; they were devotional and entomological, mainly, and he was just walking on when Layard's *Nineveh* caught his eye. He had heard young Loudon praise it. He carried it into the shop. In the shop's recesses, among washstands, horn gramophones, and rolls of linoleum, he saw the swell of a green bosom. It was a dressmaker's dummy, armless, decapitated, breastless—but not bosomless; a massive uninflected protuberance expanded above a trim waist. Below the waist the swelling hips were cut short at their maximum extension and mounted on a short pedestal, stained to imitate mahogany. The green cloth covering, a triumph of tailoring, fitted the torso as a plum skin fits a plum.

It would be the making of his party on Monday.

He carried it off, wrapped in newspapers. Though it was lighter than he expected, it proved an awkward load. The unyielding waist slipped back and forth under his arm, the pedestal bruised his hip, the newspaper fluttered and came unwrapped. Because of its rigidity, the dummy seemed larger than any normal woman could be. It was as though he were committing rape on a respectable giantess. He finished the journey by taxi.

Yet when he unwrapped it the absurdity of his purchase was forgotten. It was an inspired purchase; in one bound he had matched Marco's bland extravagance; though they should never meet again, he would have left his impression on that sweet-scented Jesus by Leonardo. Even the humblest love has savagery in it. Ronald fastened his being on the moment when he would smite astonishment into Marco as one drives in a nail.

Monday evening. Two nights from this.

For the present, the dummy had better be kept from Mrs. Palmer. This, like conveying the dummy through Camden Town, was not so easy as he expected. The same difficulty confronted him which had confronted Mr. Prothero's murderers in their hour of triumph. The wardrobe had not sufficient depth to contain her. The bed was a divan; she could not go under the bed. There was no coal cellar at his disposal. Should he make a firm parcel of her and deposit her at the Left Luggage office at Paddington Station? In the end, it seemed best to wrap her in brown paper and hoist her on top of the bookcase. It had a projecting Edwardian cornice and he knew by experience that no one dusted up there.

Twice he started from his half sleep, thinking he heard rats devouring her. Recollecting that Mrs. Palmer's cat slept on the landing, he opened his door, and later on he felt the cat walking on his bed and hollowing a place beside him. It was after that, somewhere in the timelessness of deep sleep, that he had the dream. Monday had come. Marco and the disciples and many other disciples had arrived and were dispersing themselves about the room on a dreamlike assortment of chairs, stools, sofas, and poppyhead pews. They were all glittering in fancy dress, and he himself was in a very fine dressing gown with Turkish slippers turning up at the toe. Jessamy had brought his snake in a registered envelope. It was dying, and shrunken to the size of a worm. Everyone was in high spirits; Marco played on a harp. But Ronald knew that something was wrong. His anguish swelled like a boil. He realized he had forgotten the dummy. Rising in the air, he took the parcel from the top of the bookcase and, hovering, unwrapped it, saying to himself, "If this were a dream I should find a mincing machine." But the dummy was there, and gently descending he put her in the middle of the table, pressing the pedestal into a wedding cake. Marco stared at her. His lips parted; color came into his cheeks. Slowly, he handed the harp to Ronald. Then he began to pass his hands over her, and stroked her and took her into his arms and nuzzled his head against her bosom. His veiling ringlets spread over her truncated neck, her straight back. The little knob which served to lift her by rose above his caresses. Rearing his face from her green cloth bosom, he said, "This is the only woman I could love." The disciples began to clap. The clapping swelled into thunder, turned into the cat purring. It pressed itself more closely into his warmth, yawned, and was asleep again.

It had been a rather upsetting dream and he was glad it could all be put down to the cat; even so, it resulted in his feeling out of temper with the dummy and suspecting he had made a fool of himself. Besides, what would he do with her afterward? She could not stay permanently on top of the bookcase, ousting the rolls of cartridge paper and tracing paper he kept there. He would have to explain her to Mrs. Palmer. And what explanation could he make? That he was housing her for a friend? On Monday evening, when he had completed his secret preparations, he fetched her down, unwrapped her, and placed her on the table as a centerpiece to the bottles and sausage rolls and pickled herrings and figs and doughnuts. Standing back to judge the effect, he forgot his doubts and his upsetting dream. Her stately bearing, her Edwardian contours, her assumption of the glories that were Greece, her ludicrous respectability could not fail to astonish and delight.

After the party was over, he would give her to Marco.

He sat down to wait, jumping up at intervals to alter this or improve that. It was certainly a good stroke to put the bowl of figs in front of her—an offering to a goddess. Their smolder of purple and obsidian green, their ripened curves ending in a little knob, corroborated her to perfection. It was past one in the morning. He wound his watch and went on waiting. On this occasion he was not impatient, for he was not fretting in the constraint of anxiety. All would go well. Wherever Marco was, all must go well.

His bell rang. He opened the street door on a single figure. It was Stewart's. "Come along in."

Stewart came in. He could not be offered a cigarette; he was smoking already.

"What a hot night," said Ronald, making conversation. "Sultry, really. Do sit down."

Stewart sat down. He said, "I thought I'd come along and tell you they aren't coming."

"Why, what has happened? Is anything wrong?"

They might have been drinking; they were certainly conspicuous. They were the sort of young men who lend themselves to arrest.

"Why should anything be wrong?" Stewart said. "It's just the usual. Marco's got a better invitation. Mary Brewster—she's on television—said why didn't we all go to Southend and bathe. So they all climbed in—she's got a huge car—and went. Except me. I can't swim." After a pause he added, "My head's too heavy. I sink."

As though his head were too heavy now, he sank it in his hands.

"So Marco asked you to come and tell me."

"God's teeth, no! He's got no use for that sort of thing." Stewart rolled his head between his hands. His fingers delved in his bristling hair. Dandruff flew out. "All Marco cares for is a chance to show off. And new suckers to show off to. That's why he was prancing about at Waterloo, making those poor devils sing their guts out. That's why he picked on you."

"There's no reason why I should believe this," Ronald said to himself.

Stewart, his head still between his hands, went on. "And you're lucky he's dropped you so soon, or he'd have been up to his usual games with you, needling you, driving you to the bin. He calls it his *droit du seigneur*—he says he's taking revenge on society. Now he's finished Ginger and Pickles. They aren't together any more. You're lucky to be dropped, I can tell you. Anyway, you were due to be dropped. He wasn't off your doorstep last week before he was calling you Auntie Bus Routes."

"He's been slighted," Ronald said to himself. "All this is rancor, nothing but rancor." He said aloud, "Well, I hope he's enjoying himself at Southend."

"Don't worry about that. He's enjoying himself, all right, being the life and soul of the party. *Do you know, he's almost as old as you are?*" The fury of the last sentence jerked Stewart's head out of his hands. He stared at the room. "What's that object on the table?"

"A dressmaker's dummy. I thought it would amuse Marco."

"So you bought it?—like I bought that bloody wig."

Coldly picturing how Stewart must have postured in it, his eyes imploring Marco for a crumb of attention, Ronald said,

"Well, since you're here, you'd better have something to eat. Do you like figs?"

They ate in silence and ate a great deal. Each felt a painful intimacy growing between them and hoped it would not endure. The green torso presided over the unwilled sacrament.

"Well, Stewart, you'd better be leaving. I've got to go out and get rid of this thing."

"What are you going to do with her?"

"Throw it in the canal."

Stewart said he would come too, to watch out for the spivs. "You carry her, though. You look more respectable than I do. Aren't you going to wrap her up?"

"No."

The street lamps projected their shadows, lost them, fastened them to their heels as they walked side by side. Stewart observed that it was like a funeral. Ronald made no reply. There was no one about. The hands of the clock on the public house at the corner pointed to twenty minutes to three. Autumn comes early to London. Dead leaves scuffled on the pavement—a sharp sound in the languid August night. They turned a corner and the canal extended before them. A vapor from its long tunnel attended it, curling and writhing on the surface of the water. Ronald took a grip on the dummy's waist and hurled it into the canal with all his force. There was a loud splash and it vanished. A moment later it bobbed up, sidled in the propelling ripples of its impact, heeled over, righted itself, bobbed majestically onward. They saw it heel over again, more slowly this time. The water was seeping through its cloth hide into its basketwork structure. It rolled lopsidedly, sank lower, turned turtle. Only the wooden pedestal remained in sight, with a few bubbles rising around it. Ronald had started to walk away. He walked faster and faster, and Stewart realized that there was no hope of catching up with him.

OXENHOPE

As unfailingly as one knows that the sensation of Venice is called Venice, of Ávila, Ávila, William knew that the sensation of Oxenhope was called Oxenhope. He had not been back since he was seventeen. Now he was sixty-four, and during the interval he had certainly never heard the name spoken, or spoken it himself except when he said to Isabel they might go there for their honeymoon (they went to Aix-en-Provence). He had stayed at Oxenhope for a month. Since then his life in the Consular Service had made him almost a resident in many different places; and Isabel was dead, and Isabelita married and settled in Canada, and a typhoid fever had mauled and telescoped his memories, and recovery had left him feeling like a castaway on the remainder of what life was left to him. But he could still remember every fiber of the sensation which was called Oxenhope.

The typhoid fever was not his first experience of brain-mauling. On the heels of winning a university scholarship, he discovered that all the facts he had grouped so tidily had dissolved into a broth stirred by an idiot. Evading his parents' thankful delight, he slunk away on the pretext of a walking tour. At the station in his Midland town, suddenly repossessing the name Hawick, he bought a ticket for Hawick. At Hawick he got out onto a platform raised like a bridge above a river and saw a rise of ground beyond factory chimneys. He aimed for this, and presently he was walking up a long steep hill, where there was meadowsweet growing in the ditches beside the road. As he had never known its name, he looked at it with pleasure. Some time after this an evening sky became a night sky. Unable to remember the name of a single constellation, he lay down among some heather and fell asleep. All the next day he walked, and a sensation like pleasure hovered somewhere behind his appalling consciousness of guilt, like the sun behind a fog. That afternoon, following a narrow road that wound beside a river, he saw a farmhouse on the side of a hill, and went to the door and asked for a glass of milk. He was taken into a parlor, where he sat down on a horsehair chair. The woman who brought the milk in a heavy cut-glass tumbler looked at him in silence, then went away and returned with a plate of scones. It struck him that her expression showed concern. Perhaps she was afraid of thunder. For the room had suddenly grown cold and dark, and he remembered how heavy the air had been during the last few miles and how leaden the river had lain between its green banks. He got up, thanking her, shouldering his pack and feeling for his money. "None of that," she said. "If you were a dog you shouldn't go out from here with such a storm gathering." Before he could answer, a blaze of lightning cut between them.

Like old friends they stood in the doorway watching the storm drive down the valley. Beneath it, the hills seemed shapeless and weltering as waves—those hills he was soon to know by their names, climbing them one after another and looking from their summits to other hills beyond.

All night the rain sang in the gutter pipes and clattered on the corrugated-iron roofs of the farm buildings; and sometimes another kick of lightning lit the wall where there hung a crayon copy of "The Stag at Eve." He lay in a narrow bed in an innocent room with a large white chamber pot under the table that held a ewer and basin, a painted deal chest of drawers with a crochet-edged towel laid across the top, and a small swinging mirror on a mahogany stand. Eating his supper among strangers, put to bed in a strange room, he registered nothing except his hostess's calm, large-boned face, which he saw as something irrevocably known, as though immortalized by that first lightning flash. For the rest, there was a husband, a daughter called Maggy, two sons younger than she, and three or four farm servants eating at the same table. The farm, he learned, was called Oxenhope, and behind it, deep-set in the hill, was the Oxenhope Burn.

Next morning, the woman was looking down on his awakening. He began to thank her, to apologize for having overslept. She said, "And where were you thinking of going on to?"

"Oh, nowhere in particular. Just on. I'm on a walking tour."

"A walking tour," she repeated. "Ah well, you'll be staying here for the present."

For the first few days, she organized him, telling him to write to his mother, and how to get to the post office, and how to address the postmistress, who was a bit deaf but didn't like to be reminded of it, and where to ford the river, and where to avoid the bull, and not to trust the plank bridge, and where to skirt the hornets' nest. And she gave him odd jobs to settle him—potatoes to scrape, rowanberries to pick for jelly making, knives to sharpen, peats to fetch in. When she judged him able to stand alone, she loosed him to go as he pleased.

If he had been that dog she spoke of, he would have stayed at Oxenhope for the rest of his life. He stayed for a month, bathing in the infinity of time and space. Then he went south, pleased and excited to be going to Cambridge with the scholarship he would soon outgrow as the cuckoo outgrows the nest. For his wits had come back to him and he was no longer intimidated by his learning.

One of the last things she had set him to do was to clean up the family gravestones, lending him a bicycle to cover the eight miles between the farm and the kirk, equipping him with a knife to pick the lichen out of the inscriptions and a toothbrush to brush it away with. It had been a cheerful morning's work, listening to the curlews and the minister's conversational hens, with the wind bringing him the noise of the river from time to time, and he had made a good job of it, so that he took credit to himself—a step back to his rational man.

But it must be a long time now since anyone had cleaned the gravestones.

It took him longer than he expected to find them. As he drove up the valley it seemed to him that it was even more sparsely populated than he remembered. The increase was in the population of the dead. Assuring himself that by now she must be dead, he had not allowed for all the others whom time had raked there and laid in close rows. He was beginning to think she might still be alive when he found himself looking at her name: Helen Sword, Wife to Robert Scott of Oxenhope. She had died in 1942, her husband five years after her. The curlews were crying, the wind was in the same quarter, but blowing more steadily, so that the noise of the river poured into his ears. He took out his knife and began to scratch at her encrusted name. The chiseling was shallow and imprecise compared to that of the earlier names above hers and on the two other stones. It was as if by this date there was not the same expectation of being remembered. A tradesman's van went up the valley as he worked and was back again, so it seemed, in a whisk. Eight miles was not so long as it had been. The Renault 1100 would take him to Oxenhope while his mind was still delaying as to whether or no he would stop at the gate.

It was his mind that carried him past it and on. As the road shook off the manse's windbreak fir plantations and the bare narrowing valley extended before him, he began to boil like a pot in the ecstasy of recognition. There, on the slope of Singlee Knowe, was the dry-stone sheepfold with the dark ring of nettles round it like the woolwork mat under a potted plant. There was the rushy field where the floods carried the hay before the haymakers could. There was the line of crouching alders beside the Drum Pool, and the flashing shoal beyond it. There, under the outcropping of rock, was the boggy cleft where he had found grass-of-Parnassus. There, like a wrinkle on a shaven cheek, was the Oxenhope Burn fissuring the hillside. He drove over the bridge (it was almost too narrow for his car) and past the house, only noticing that the porch was gone and that the herd's cottage had a television mast. The road dwindled on ahead, turning to a grassy track where groups of sheep were feeding. He slowed the car to a standstill. They did not move away. When he sounded his horn they turned their pale fanatic faces toward him, and the foremost of them stamped his hoof pettishly once or twice and then fell to feeding again. Suddenly, for no apparent reason, they all turned and bolted up the hillside. Half a mile farther on he came to another group of sheep, who behaved in identically the same way, and he recalled Jimmie Laidlaw, the Scotts' shepherd, remarking that sheep were very regulated animals. For a moment it seemed that Jimmie's actual voice was creaking and whirring in his ears. He sometimes used to find that he heard too much of it; Jimmie, because of his solitary calling, was like an uncorked bottle when he came on a hearer. He talked about sheep, and hard winters, and a black dog that dragged a coffin over Cold Face on Old Year's Night, and a sheepfold that moved with the solstice, so that every time you came to it the opening was a little farther round; and of wildcats, and Covenanters, and lights hovering above the water, moving and staying as the current carried the drowned body, lodged it against an obstacle, worked it free again; and of cholera, and the itch, and an ash tree that cured rickets. But now he rather wished Jimmie would come with his slow shepherd's trudge along the track. Jimmie with his memory extending in all directions was one of those people who need never die; and he would answer questions about Maggy and the two boys, and what changes the unchanging valley had seen, and who was at the post office in these days. But all these questions William could ask later on, and have them anwered or not; they were husks of the past, no more.

The past was in the present—the narrowed valley, the steeper hills crowding into it, the river running with a childish voice. On from the junction with the Aila Burn it was scarcely a river at all—just a winding green morass, speechless unless you sank your foot in it. So on the day when he had set out to track the river to its head it was natural that he should have followed the tributary Aila Burn, that ran in a deep crevice, like the Oxenhope Burn, but more steeply. Hauling himself up from waterfall to waterfall, here by a rowan, there by handfuls of heather, he had come to a pool, wide enough to swim a few strokes across, deep enough—though it was so clear that its pebbles seemed within hand's reach—to take him up to the neck. He had stripped and bathed in the ice-cold water, threshing about like a kelpie, and then clambered out on a slab of rock to dry in the sun. He had lain so still in his happiness that after a while an adder elongated itself from the heather roots, lowered the poised head with its delicate, tranquil features, and basked on the rock beside him. There they had lain till a hawk's shadow crossed them, and with a flick the adder was gone.

He could not hope to climb the Aila Burn this time, but for love of the adder he would press the car on till he came within earshot of its waterfalls.

He got out and went as far as the first waterfall, because, like an epicure, he wanted to drink the water at its coldest and most elemental. It thrust into his hand and out again, drenching his sleeve. The plunge of the water into the pool,

the stone, mottled like a trout, which it incessantly broke its
sleek neck on, the renewed surface, fanning out and smoothly
hastening away—he recognized everything. Other recognitions
were everywhere around him, tingling in rocks, in soggy
patches at the rocks' foot, in the shadow of a hill moving
across another hill, in tufts of sheep's wool caught on wire
fencing, in the wind's hoo-hooing in the crannies of stone
walls, in the seething hiss of dried heather bells. A grouse
caught sight of him and cried out, "Go-back, go-back, go-
back!" But the adjuration was beside the point. The past was
in the present, and he was back. Where next? If he could not
climb, he could walk. Even without deciding, he knew: another drink from the Aila Burn, a ham sandwich in the car;
then, circling up the heathery shoulder of Phawp Law, to the
Cat Loch. Even if he could not get all the way, he would at
least go far enough to look down on it, as he had done on that
astonishing first sight. For when one's last backward glance at
a river showed it no wider than a skein of darning wool, one
does not expect to see a lake lying on the knees of the hills, a
lake with nothing running into it or draining out of it, yet
complete with a boathouse.

On a later occasion he was to push out of that boathouse—
an experience that would have been a solemn rapture if it had
not been for the company of Oliphant, the keeper. Oliphant
was a harmless enough fellow, but Levitical, and bent on making it clear he wasn't a native. It was for this reason that
Major Baxter could allow him to take a rod on the loch from
time to time: "I can trust you not to take out more than three
of the trout." The trout were pink-fleshed and, like Oliphant,
imported from elsewhere. He was punctilious in seeing that
William should have the first casts and polite in saying he was
doing well, that all he needed was a little practice. With the
fatality of beginners, William caught a fish. It wasn't a large
one, but Oliphant netted it as ceremoniously as if it had been
a salmon, and killed it by knocking its head against the side

of the boat. It went on leaping galvanically, long after—
which, according to Oliphant, proved its lineage. They fished
on, but it was the only fish they caught.

He had remembered the height of Phawp Law more or less
accurately; but he had forgotten to allow for its bulk. Even
when the skyline had no more tricks to play on him there was
a great stretch of ground to cover. The climb had dizzied him;
he had no impetus left. He could only walk by small
ambitions—as far as the tuft of rushes, thence on to a farther
tuft, thence on under the jut of a peat hag, thence over an expanse of burned and bristling heather. Watching his steps, he
was in full sight of the loch before he saw it. It lay in its au-
reole of rainbow grass and was the same rather sullen blue—
the blue of bog water. The boathouse, however, was gone.

Well, there was the Cat Loch, intact and solitary and self-
possessing. The blur of Oliphant and Major Baxter and
himself had been wiped off it, like breath off a mirror. No one
fished there now, unless it were a heron. He sat down and listened to his mind making fragmentary remarks, spaced among
his gasps for breath. An uncommonly silly heron. No sensible
heron . . . would come so far . . . on the chance of spiking a
fish on that shelving rim. "Old herons go a-fishing there." . . .
Odd, when you come to think of it, that in popular speech the
word "old" is used as a semiendearment. Not so endearing
when you have to nail it into the lonely flesh. He went on listening to his mind's limping trivialities, sheltering against the
moment when he would have to admit that the past was
draining away out of the present, that Oxenhope, lovely as
ever, was irrecoverable, that he would never possess the sensation of Oxenhope again. He had grasped at the substance, and
the lovely shadow was lost. For suppose it were possible to implement that sketchy project of finding a house in the valley
and ending his days there—what would he do? Take himself
out for walks, record the weather in a notebook, suck a rowan-

berry in autumn, huddle his old bones through the long winters, wonder if he would smell the summer heather again and find the grass-of-Parnassus? He looked at his watch. It had taken him ninety minutes to get here. Another ninety minutes would see him down. He would get into the car and drive away and be at the hotel in time for dinner. As incontrovertibly as she had said, "You'll be staying here for the present," the loch said, "You'll be away by tomorrow."

He was stirring to get to his feet when he knew, as an animal does, that he was being watched; and like an animal, he became motionless. It was an intense scrutiny: no sheep watches one so; perhaps it was a weasel. Sliding his glance in the direction of the watcher, he saw two brilliant pink flowers lighting a clump of heather: two outstanding ears with the sun shining through them. The boy had concealed himself very well, but his ears betrayed him.

If I had been that boy, thought William, I would have wished the unsuspecting stranger to go away and leave me to trail him. And after a decency-pause he did his part in the transaction. The boy had more strategy than to follow him across the stretch of burned heather. A hare starting up the slope showed that he must have taken a lower course, parallel to William's. Later, a couple of sheep were disturbed. Later still, the boy began to run at full tilt down the remainder of the hillside, dislodging stones, swishing through bracken, leaving a track of sound behind him. When William was down and approaching his car along the grassed road, he saw the boy approaching it from the opposite direction. Though his ears were no longer translucent, they were certainly the same ears.

The sun had left the valley, and the snipe flickered like shadows over the green of the damp grass. The air was full of chill and poetry, and it was the moment to put on an overcoat. Ignoring the boy, who was now standing by the car without appearing to have stopped there, William leaned in and released the lid of the bonnet. The boy started back as he raised it, and exclaimed, "Mercy!"

"The engine is at the back."

"Oh, aye."

"Would you like to look at it?"

"Aye."

The boy examined the engine carefully but without passion. Clearly, his proper study was man.

"Would you like a lift down the valley?"

"I wouldna mind," said the boy, falling into the trap.

"Where do you live?"

"At Crosscleugh."

Having by his countertrap established that William was not a total stranger to the valley, the boy became hospitable. "Yon's Carra Law," he said. "Yon's Cold Face."

William looked at the one and the other with attention.

"Yon's Scraggie Law. There was a man once, put goats on it. They were Spanish goats. They didna do."

"One couldn't expect it."

"This is the Aila Burn," the boy continued. "There's a pool halfway up it, no bigger than a barrel. But it's deep. Once it drowned six sheep. There was a snowstorm and they fell in. Then they couldna get out. The burn ran red with blood—the way they fought each other with their feet."

William had heard that story from Jimmie Laidlaw. "What's that hill?"

"That's just Phawp Law."

They looked at each other sternly.

"There's a loch away up there," the boy said. "It's called the Cat Loch."

"Why is it called the Cat Loch?"

"I couldna say. Something to do with a cat, maybe." A vision transfigured his face as the sun had transfigured his ears. "There was a man once, set fire to it. He was in a boat, and he set fire to the water. There was flames coming up all round the boat. Like a gas ring."

Oliphant, interminably rowing about the loch for likely places, had thrust down his oar to check the boat's movement. Bubbles of marsh gas rose to the surface. William saw himself leaning out of the boat and touching off their tiny incandescence with a lighted match.

"What color were the flames?" he asked.

"They were blue."

"Jump in," William said briskly, and turned the car. When the surface allowed, he drove fast, to please the boy. He put him down at Crosscleugh (there was still a white marble dog in the garden) and drove on. There was no call for a backward glance, for an exile's farewell. He had his tenancy in legend. He was secure.